'I didn't take anything!' A
'Anyway, Sarah said it
pretended he believed me

Jack gritted his teeth.

'Can you blame him?' he shouted at her. 'You're saying you've got an invisible friend from the twenty-fifth century who goes around stealing from people who annoy you, to teach them a lesson, and we're expected to believe you! Come off it, Annie! We all know it's you!'

Annie glanced across at 'Sarah', as if she was listening to her, and then looked back at her brother. 'Prove it,' she said with a little smile.

ANNIE'S GAME

A CORGI YEARLING BOOK : 0 440 864011
First publication in Great Britain

PRINTING HISTORY
Corgi Yearling edition published 1999

Set in 12/14.5pt Century Schoolbook by
Phoenix Typesetting, Ilkley, West Yorkshire

Corgi Yearling Books are published by Transworld Publishers Ltd,
61–63 Uxbridge Road, Ealing, London W5 5SA,
in Australia by Transworld Publishers (Australia) Pty. Ltd,
15–25 Helles Avenue, Moorebank, NSW 2170,
and in New Zealand by Transworld Publishers (NZ) Ltd,
3 William Pickering Drive, Albany, Auckland.

Made and printed in Great Britain by
Cox & Wyman Ltd, Reading, Berkshire

Annie's Game

Game

Narinder Dhami

CORGI YEARLING BOOKS

For Robert

CHAPTER ONE

Annie was talking to someone who wasn't there.

Jack looked across the school playground at his sister. She was nodding her head and smiling at the empty space next to her, waving her hands around as she talked. Jack wondered briefly why he was surprised. Nothing Annie did ought to surprise him any more. She was capable of anything, including having a conversation with thin air. Not that he cared what Annie was up to. All he was concerned about was getting his sister well out of the way, so he could try to overhear what their mother was saying to Mr Daniels. Something was going on. Jack was sure of it. Their mother had been acting strangely for the last week or so now, and he was determined to find out the reason why.

'Annie!' he called. 'Go and sit on the wall.'

Annie gave him a big smile.

'*Por que*?'

'Speak English, can't you?' Since Annie had taught herself Spanish, she'd increased her ability to irritate by 100 per cent.

Annie shrugged. 'I said: "Why?"'

'Because I say so.' Jack glanced up at the open windows of Mr Daniels' office on the second floor. He could hear voices. Their mother had been talking to the headmaster for a few minutes already, and he didn't want to waste any more time.

'Can Sarah come with me?'

'What?' Jack turned back to his sister.

'I said, "Can Sarah come with me?"'

'Sarah who?'

'Sarah Slade.' Annie pointed at the empty space next to her, a pleased look on her face. 'This is Sarah. She's my new friend. Say hello to Sarah, Jack.'

'There's no-one there,' Jack muttered.

'Yes, there is,' Annie retorted, unruffled. 'She's just invisible, that's all.'

'Of course she is,' said Jack. 'Silly me. I should have realized.'

'Don't be sarcastic, Jack.' Annie opened her

eyes wide, and gave him a superior stare. 'Sarah's a time-traveller, you know. She's come to visit me from the future.'

Jack resisted a desire to bang his head against the nearest brick wall. It was a feeling he often had when he was left alone with Annie.

'Look,' he said, unable to stand any more of what threatened to be yet another of Annie's endless games, 'go over there and sit on the wall. Have you got something to read?'

Annie pouted. 'I'd rather talk to Sarah.'

Jack looked at her sternly. 'Have you got something to read?' he repeated.

Annie sighed. 'I've got two newspapers, four comics and *Hamlet*.'

'*Hamlet*? You mean *Hamlet* by William Shakespeare?' Again Jack wondered why he was surprised. Annie had been reading the *Financial Times* last week, and telling their mother the price of Marks and Spencer shares. Shakespeare was the next logical step.

Annie nodded enthusiastically. 'It's good,' she said. 'It's about this man who—'

'Never mind.' Jack took his sister's hand, and marched her over to the low wall that separated the playground from the football pitch. 'Just sit there and read.'

Annie clicked her heels together, and saluted him. 'Yes, sir!'

Jack felt his lips twitch, but he didn't smile. If you smiled, Annie took that as encouragement, and then there was no stopping her. He turned away.

Annie sat down on the wall, and opened her little pink rucksack.

'Sarah says, were you born a bossy-boots, or did you have to practise?' she called after him.

Jack looked back over his shoulder to make a cutting remark. But before he had a chance to say anything, he tripped and went flying. With a yelp of surprise, he thought fast, and instinctively managed to fling out his hands just in time to stop his whole body from thumping down onto the hard surface of the playground.

Behind him, Annie started to giggle. 'Sarah, that's naughty!' As Jack picked himself up, she grinned cheekily at him. 'Sarah says it serves you right.'

Jack dusted off his hands, gritted his teeth and walked off. Did anyone in the whole of the known universe have a five-year-old sister like his? Somehow he didn't think so.

The school day had finished some fifteen minutes earlier, and everyone had gone, so the playground was empty. Most of the teachers must have gone too, because there were hardly any cars left in the car park. Jack still looked round cautiously, though, checking carefully in every direction. The only people he could see were some boys from his own class. Bonehead Griffiths and his gang were playing football in the road outside the playground, but because there was a punch-up over some alleged foul every few minutes, they weren't taking any notice of him.

As he walked over to stand underneath the headmaster's window, Jack reckoned that he was pretty safe. That didn't stop him from feeling nervous. He tried to stop feeling nervous by telling himself that some kids wouldn't think twice about doing something like this. Somebody like Bonehead Griffiths, for instance, wouldn't bat an eyelid. Bonehead Griffiths, the hard man of Mansfield Primary, would listen in to any of the teachers' conversations without compunction, and then try to sell the information round the school. But this was the first time that Jack had ever done anything of this kind.

It had been a warm day, so all the windows of the headmaster's office were wide open. Jack told himself silently that if the conversation was really and truly private, Daniels would have closed the windows. That eased his conscience just a bit. Frowning, he leaned against the wall, and tuned in to what his mum was saying.

'. . . and I just wanted to find out if things have

improved since I last spoke to you.' Jack could hear the open anxiety in his mother's voice. He knew she was worried about Annie. But there was something else going on. He was sure of it. 'How's Annie getting on in class now? Have there been any improvements?'

'Well, broadly speaking, the situation is still as it was the last time we met.' Mr Daniels cleared his throat, and there was a pause of at least five seconds. 'Annabel is still refusing to speak English in class, and insists on speaking Spanish instead. As her teacher, Miss Turner, doesn't actually speak Spanish, this does create rather a disturbance.'

Jack grinned to himself. Mr Daniels wasn't wrong there. Miss Turner had turned into a nervous wreck, who was practically chain-smoking her way from class to staffroom.

His mother sighed.

'She does that at home sometimes,' she said. 'She only started teaching herself Spanish about three months ago, and she's already fluent. She's threatened to start Russian next.'

Mr Daniels sighed too, perhaps inwardly debating whether to send Miss Turner on a Modern Languages course. Jack felt vindicated. He found it very satisfying to know that not even grown-ups seemed to be able to cope with his sister very well.

'It's certainly not making her teacher's life very easy,' the headmaster said carefully. 'If Annie could just be persuaded to speak English in class, I'm sure she and Miss Turner would get on a lot better.'

'I've talked to Annie about it over and over again, but she's not just being cheeky, you know,' Jack's mother said quickly. 'She lives in a world of her own. Half the time she doesn't know what she's doing.'

Jack shook his head. He didn't agree with his mother on that one. In his opinion, Annie knew exactly what she was doing. She might only be five years old, but she had the brains and the ability to wind everyone up to perfection.

'I'm sorry to keep going on about this, Mr Daniels, but as I said to you when Annie started school, I really don't want her to be made to feel odd or strange.' His mother had lowered her voice now, and Jack had to strain his ears to catch the words. 'Of course she knows she's different, but I want her to fit in with the other kids here as much as possible.'

Fit in? Jack repeated the words silently and scornfully to himself. Fit in? Annie stood out at Mansfield Primary like a Big Mac at a vegetarian dinner. Their mother's mission in life had always been to try and make Annie seem as ordinary and normal as possible, but Annie wasn't ordinary, she wasn't normal and she'd never 'fit in' at Mansfield Primary if she stayed there till she was ninety-five.

Annie had only started at Mansfield four or five weeks ago, and everyone there knew what she was like. It had been all over the school within five minutes of her walking into the Reception classroom. The novelty of having an infant prodigy in the school had not yet worn off, either. Jack was still being asked countless times a day what it was like to have a sister who was almost seven years younger than he was, and seven million times smarter. Of course, people like Bonehead Griffiths and his gang had taken a malicious glee in turning the knife in the wound. But children Jack had thought were his friends had commented on it too, not realizing that it was a sensitive subject, and even – and this had especially got up Jack's nose – some of the teachers. Did they think he didn't realize just how many light years ahead of him Annie was? It had only been rammed down his throat from the time Annie had started talking at only six months old.

'Annie seems to be a bit of a loner, and that worries me as well,' his mother was saying. 'I was wondering if she'd made any friends yet.'

No chance, Jack said silently to himself. Mr Daniels didn't put it quite so bluntly.

'Well, I've asked Miss Turner to try and make sure that Annie has plenty of opportunities to mix with the other children in her class,' the headmaster said slowly. 'But it's early days yet. And of course,' he cleared his throat again, 'none of the other children in Annie's class speak Spanish either, so communication seems to be a little limited.'

Jack rolled his eyes. This whole situation was so ridiculous, it was almost funny.

'The problem is obviously that Annabel is bored,' Mr Daniels went on. 'She finds the work in the Reception class far too easy, and spends most of her time translating reading books into Spanish. However, what I can do, Mrs Robinson, is give you a little more information about the special arrangements that the school is making for Annabel's education.' Jack heard the noise of papers being rustled. 'We're still in discussion with the local education authority about the best course of action to take. Obviously Annie's already far in advance of the other children in the Reception class in all subjects, so, while we decide exactly what would be best for her, we're considering allowing her to take some lessons with the Year Four and Year Five children.'

Not with his Year Six class then, Jack noted with relief. Imagine the humiliation of having his baby sister sitting in on his classes, and getting all the answers right as well. It just didn't bear thinking about.

'I'm not sure I want her put in with the older children,' his mother said doubtfully. 'To be honest, I'm a lot more concerned at the moment about how Annie's fitting in at school socially, with kids of her own age.'

'Well, let's give it a couple of months and see what happens, shall we?' Jack could detect a slight note of desperation in the headmaster's voice. He got the distinct impression that Daniels had probably never come across another pupil quite like Annie in his life before, and that he didn't know quite how to handle her either. 'Having her older brother at the school already should help Annie settle in over the next few months.'

'And Jack's getting on all right, isn't he?'

Suddenly alert, Jack looked up at the open window.

'Yes, of course, Mrs Robinson. Jack's a very bright boy.'

Wait for it, Jack told himself, curling his lip cynically. Here it comes. That all-important 'but'.

'But of course he isn't an exceptionally intelligent and gifted child like Annabel.' The knife turned in the wound yet again, even though Jack knew it was ridiculous to feel hurt. He ought to

16

be used to it by now. After all, he'd had to hear comments like that almost every day of his life so far. And he'd probably have to hear comments like that every day until he dropped down dead. Annie would always be cleverer than he was, and he had no chance of catching her up, ever. The thought depressed him.

'When you phoned up to arrange the appointment, you mentioned something about the children's father . . . ?'

Jack stiffened at the headmaster's words. Why were Daniels and his mother raking all that up again? His father had been gone for almost four years now, he hadn't phoned or written or visited in all that time. Something hard and bitter twisted his heart deep inside him. Their father had left just ten months after Annie was born.

'Well, to tell you the truth, Mr Daniels, that's the main reason why I wanted to see you today.'

Jack's heart began to thump hugely inside his chest. Suddenly he sensed that something important was coming, maybe the very thing he'd been waiting to find out.

'The children's father phoned me last week from the States, completely out of the blue. He hasn't been in touch for three or four years, and now this. I haven't told the kids yet, and I'm not sure if I'm going to. With Annie having so many problems at school at the moment, I don't want to unsettle her even more.'

His father had got in touch. At last. Jack began to shake all over with an emotion that spilled slowly, and then with increasing force, right from the centre of him. But before he had time even to touch on the implications of what his mum had said, the hairs on the back of his neck prickled, and he sensed that there was someone standing behind him. Hoping it wasn't a teacher, he spun round.

'Annie!' he hissed furiously. 'What d'you think you're doing?'

Annie was staring up at him solemnly, her brown eyes as round as buttons.

'Sarah says it's rude to listen to other people's conversations.'

'Shut up, and go and sit down!' Jack mouthed at her. Annie shrugged and turned away, her arm stuck out stiffly by her side, as if she was holding hands with someone who wasn't there. Jack watched her go back across the playground, his heart banging so loudly he was surprised Mr Daniels couldn't hear it. He wasn't sure if Annie had heard what their mum had said, but even if she had, it didn't matter. Annie could hardly remember their dad, so why should she care? It was Jack who would be most affected by what he'd just heard.

He let out a long breath of relief, so long it felt as if he'd been holding it in for the last four years. For the first time, he allowed his mind to slip back to the day his father had left. For years he'd pushed the memory away, digging a deep hole in the back of his mind and burying it there. Now, gently, he let it swim to the surface again. He remembered his father going down the path with his saxophone case in one hand and his suitcase in the other. The taxi had been waiting by the kerb with the engine running. It had sounded impatient, as if it couldn't wait to whisk his father away to the airport, and a new life in America. Jack had been pressed up against the window, watching him go. He could remember the feel of the glass against his face as he watched, smooth and cold and wet with tears. His mother had never explained exactly why his father had left, and Jack had never asked her. He didn't have to. He'd always known that it was because of Annie.

'What do you think you're doing there, Robinson?' hissed a voice in Jack's ear.

Jack leapt a mile. Nicko was standing close beside him, grinning at him, and bouncing a football up and down with one hand.

'Sssh!' Quickly Jack grabbed the ball before it hit the ground again, and jerked his head upwards. 'My mum's up there with Daniels.'

'What for?' Nicko asked curiously, then he grinned. 'No, don't tell me.' He put his hands either side of his head, about twenty centimetres away from his ears. 'It's the Egghead, isn't it?'

Jack shrugged.

'Sort of . . .' Some things were too private to discuss, even with your best mate. At least until you'd had time to sort them out in your own mind first.

Nicholas Hamilton was Jack's best friend. His family had moved into the Robinsons' street a year or two back, and Jack had got to know him the very day they'd arrived. He'd taken Annie to the corner shop to buy some ice cream and, on their way back home, they'd walked past Nicko, who'd been standing morosely in the front garden, kicking the lawn. Annie had looked at him and said in her precise voice, 'Hello. Do you know what the capital city of Peru is?'

She was three years old at the time, and obsessed with looking at maps of the world.

Nicko had done a complete double-take. 'Er – no,' he'd said warily, obviously wondering if this was some kind of test that anyone new to the street had to pass. 'Do you?'

'Yes, of course I do.' Annie had beamed at him kindly. 'It's Lima.'

Nicko had stared at Jack, his eyes round with

delight, and said, 'Cool! Egghead or what!' and they'd been friends ever since.

Jack gave Nicko the ball back, and he tucked it under one arm.

'I thought everyone had gone home,' Jack whispered.

'I've been home, I was on my way to the shop when I saw you lurking around in the playground,' Nicko whispered back. 'Want to come?'

'Can't.' Jack nodded his head in Annie's direction.

'Got to baby-sit, have you?' Nicko squinted across the playground at Annie. 'What's that she's reading? *Omlet?* What is it, a cookery book?'

'Put your glasses on, dummy,' Jack said as quietly as he could between giggles. Nicko was supposed to wear spectacles, but he hated them and kept them in his pocket all day. Jack had lost count of the number of times Nicko had lost them or sat on them. 'It's *Hamlet* by William Shakespeare.'

'Oh, right,' Nicko said casually. Then his eyes widened. 'What, *the* William Shakespeare?'

'The very same.' Jack heard the sound of the windows being closed overhead, and, panicking in case Mr Daniels spotted them lurking underneath, he grabbed Nicko's arm. The two boys flattened themselves against the wall for a few seconds, and then they legged it safely across the playground to the wall where Annie was sitting.

'That was close,' Jack muttered, his heart pounding. Still, he'd found out what he'd wanted to know. Now he didn't know whether he was glad or sorry. He was glad his father had got in touch, of course he was. But what was going to happen now?

Annie looked up from *Hamlet,* and pouted.

'I'm hungry,' she said in a whiny voice. 'When are we going home?'

'When mum's finished talking to Daniels,' Jack snapped at her. He needed to take his frustration out on someone, and Annie was always an easy target. 'And this is your fault. If you hadn't been speaking Spanish to your teacher all the time, we wouldn't be hanging around here now.'

Annie turned a page of her book, looking unconcerned.

'Miss Turner should look up what I say in the dictionary,' she said. 'That's what they're there for.'

'Oh yeah?' Nicko grinned at her. 'And what if everybody in your class suddenly started speaking a different language? What would poor old Miss Turner do then?'

Annie giggled with delight. She liked Nicko. He always talked to her as if she was

22

a real person, and he didn't assume that she was being deliberately odd. Not like her brother . . .

'That is illogical, Captain,' she said to Nicko, with a big grin on her face.

'Hey, is that Shakespeare?' Nicko asked, looking over Annie's shoulder at *Hamlet*.

'Don't be a dummy,' Jack said shortly. 'She's into *Star Trek* at the moment as well.'

'Yeah?' Nicko looked impressed. 'Shakespeare and *Star Trek*. Cool.'

'No, it isn't,' said Jack. 'She knows all the episodes off by heart, and she keeps on repeating them from start to finish. It drives me crazy.'

Annie closed her book, put it down on the wall and looked her brother up and down, an evil glint in her eye. 'It's life, Jim, but not as we know it.'

Nicko burst out laughing. Jack didn't even smile. It was all right for Nicko. *He* didn't have to put up with a five-year-old genius all the time. Life with Annie was hell, and always had been.

Although he was angry with his father for leaving, Jack didn't really blame him. From the age of about six months, Annie had been impossible. She had been crawling at seven months and walking at nine months, and she was into everything. She had been, and still was, as inquisitive as a squirrel. When their father had found her trying to take his CD player apart, they'd put everything movable they owned into the loft, to keep it, and Annie, safe. For a year or two, the house had looked as empty as if they'd been burgled.

Annie had been hyperactive, hardly sleeping, hardly stopping, always on the go. She had also learnt to talk rapidly, going from single words to grammatically correct sentences at high speed, obviously fascinated by language and her ability to communicate. But, with her incredible intelligence still in advance of her language skills, she had screamed and screamed with frustration if she couldn't find the words to say exactly what she wanted. Jack had horrific memories of screaming fits that seemed to last for days, even weeks. Another of Annie's most annoying habits when she was learning to talk, and one which drove Jack and his parents to distraction, was the way she latched onto a word or phrase, and kept on repeating it for hours, rolling the words round and round on her tongue as if she was savouring them like food. Once she'd heard someone in *EastEnders* say, 'Leave it to me. I'll get it sorted,' and she'd kept on saying it and saying it, until their mother had locked herself in the bathroom and broken down.

Then, as Annie quickly grew more and more fluent, the questions had started. Endless,

endless questions. They were always questions Jack and his parents didn't know the answers to as well, like why is the sun round and not triangular or square, and why is grass green, and not blue or yellow or red, and why can't we see the wind. In despair, their mother had spent pounds on expensive encyclopaedias, so that Annie could look up the answers to her questions herself. But that still didn't stop Annie from talking, talking, talking from morning till night. Her mind, and her mouth, seemed inexhaustible.

So Jack didn't blame his father for leaving. Not much, anyway. If he could have left himself, he probably would have.

'So,' Nicko went to squat on the wall, next to Annie. 'What's the story with this Hamlet dude then?'

'Don't sit there!' Annie yelled at the top of her lungs, pushing him away. Nicko leapt a mile as if he'd been stung, and stared at her, open-mouthed.

'Why not?'

Annie nodded at the wall next to her. 'Sarah's sitting there,' she said.

Nicko looked nervously at the empty space, then glanced at Jack. Jack shrugged, and mouthed, 'One of her daft games,' at him. Nicko squinted at him, trying to lip-read. Jack did it again, and this time Annie spotted him.

'My games are *not* daft,' she said haughtily. 'And anyway, this isn't a game, it's real. This is Sarah Slade.' She pointed at the empty space next to her. 'Go on, Nicko, say hello to Sarah.'

'Hello, Sarah,' Nicko said obediently. Jack kept quiet. After all that had happened so far today, he needed this like a hole in the head.

'Sarah says hi.' Annie smiled at Nicko. 'She likes *you*. Not like some rude people she could mention.' She looked accusingly at her brother.

Jack turned away from her. 'Leave me out of it,' he muttered.

Annie's games always drove him crazy, and he could see no reason why this one should be any different. His sister was always inventing games. Not ordinary, normal games like other kids made up, but complicated, imaginary projects that only she could keep track of. She wrote notes about them in exercise books and drew maps and made models, until she got bored with the current game, and started a new one. Her last game had involved a prince and a princess, a mad wizard and a blue tiger called Gerald, and she'd invented a whole imaginary country to go with it, including a made-up language which was a mixture of Spanish and English words, pronounced backwards.

'Who's Sarah then?' Nicko asked curiously.

'Sarah's eleven years old, and she's a time-traveller from the twenty-fifth century.' Annie beamed at him.

'Is that right?' Nicko looked over Annie's head, and winked at Jack. 'What's she doing here then?'

'She's doing a school project on the 1990s, and she's come to do some research,' Annie explained, her face serious.

'Groovy.' Nicko raised his eyebrows. 'So they still have schools in the twenty-fifth century, do they? Still, time-travelling to research a history project sounds a lot more interesting than sitting in a boring old library.'

'And she's sitting right there,' Jack said suddenly, pointing at the empty space next to Annie.

Annie nodded eagerly. She loved it when her brother took an interest in her games. Not that he often did.

'Let's see then, shall we?' Jack said with an evil grin, and he sat down quickly next to Annie.

He wasn't quite sure what happened next. One second he was sitting on the wall, and the next he'd overbalanced and gone heels over head onto the grass behind it, landing with a loud thud. Gasping with shock, he pulled himself upright to find Nicko and Annie peering down at him. Annie was grinning smugly and Nicko was very red in the face as if he was trying not to laugh.

'Serves you right,' Annie said cheerfully. 'I *told* you Sarah was sitting there.'

Jack stood up painfully. It *did* serve him right, he thought sourly. It served him right for getting involved in Annie's stupid game in the first place. Trust him to go and overbalance, just when he was trying to show her how daft she was being with this Sarah Slade rubbish.

'Look, Nicko, we've got to go,' he muttered as he saw their mum coming across the playground towards them. 'See you tomorrow.'

'OK.' Nicko grinned at Annie. 'Bye, Annie.' Then he waved at the empty space as he walked off. 'Bye, Sarah.'

Annie giggled, and Jack rolled his eyes in irritation. Nicko was always encouraging her, and it was time he stopped.

'Come on, let's go home.' Their mother looked exhausted, and Jack stared at her anxiously. How long would it be before she told him that their dad had been in touch? Would she tell him at all? Because Nicko had come along, he hadn't heard what Mr Daniels had said when their mother had asked his advice. Had Daniels told her to keep quiet for a while, in case it upset Annie?

Their mum picked *Hamlet* up off the wall, and slid it into her handbag without comment.

'Shall we stop on the way, and pick up a pizza, kids?'

'Goody!' Annie jumped up, and ran to hold her mother's hand. Jack followed behind them, wondering for the millionth time if he'd ever come anywhere near to understanding his little sister. There she was calmly reading *Hamlet* five minutes ago, and now she was holding their mum's hand, and telling her she didn't want olives or onions on her pizza. It was something Jack just couldn't get his head round, so he didn't bother trying. It was like living with a Martian.

After they'd got home and he'd had some pizza, Jack went straight up to his bedroom to be on his own. He switched on his computer and then immediately switched it off again, feeling too restless to do anything. Pity there wasn't a computer game called *How to Cope with Finding Your Missing Father*, Jack thought sardonically, flopping onto the bed. 'Experience the lows of rejection when your father walks out on you! Feel the thrilling excitement of that first phone call after nothing for three-and-a-half years! Fight your way through ten levels of emotion, and win through to a Happy Ever After Ending!' Maybe he ought to write his own computer program. After all, he had all the relevant experience.

He lay there, thinking for a while. Then abruptly he got up, got down on his hands and knees and peered under the bed. He hadn't looked under there for a long, long time. Taking a deep breath, Jack reached into the dark, dusty space, and groped around until he found what he was looking for. It was right at the back, where he'd shoved it years ago.

The case was blue, but it looked almost grey because it was covered in dust. Jack wiped it clean with his sleeve, and undid the locks, feeling his heartbeat quicken. The saxophone was still there, fitting neatly into the cut-out holes in the blue velvet.

It had been his dad's. Not his best instrument, the one he used when he was working, but one of his old ones. He'd started teaching Jack to play it just before he left, and Jack had never taken it out of its case since.

Suddenly he slammed the case shut, sending dust flying everywhere and making his eyes water. He pushed it back under the bed, his throat burning with tears of frustration. He couldn't very well do or say anything until his mother told him officially that his dad had been in touch. He'd just have to wait and see what happened.

'Jack?' That was his mum, calling up from

downstairs. 'Will you check that Annie's in bed please?'

Jack got up, and went out onto the landing. There was no dust out there, but his eyes were still watering, and he had to blink hard to clear them.

Annie's room was a tip. The floor was covered with card and coloured paper, bits of string and Sellotape, felt pens and crayons, pictures cut out of magazines and pots of paint, and pieces of paper covered in writing and diagrams. In the middle of it sat Annie in her pyjamas, a pair of scissors in her hand.

'Time for bed,' Jack said abruptly, not even bothering to comment on the mess as he picked his way carefully over to the window. He was used to Annie's games taking over. The last model she'd made had been the mad wizard's castle, an enormous, complicated cardboard model with every room, tower and turret carefully labelled and built to scale from a detailed plan, but now that had been crumpled up and jammed head-first into the waste-paper basket.

'Mind out, Sarah's sitting on the window sill,' Annie said, as Jack pulled the curtains together. Jack ignored her.

'Look, I've made a model of Sarah's house.

That's what houses are going to look like in the twenty-fifth century. Sarah told me so.'

Jack glanced without interest at a couple of cereal cartons painted silver and glued on top of each other.

'Come on. Bed.'

Reluctantly Annie put down her scissors, and picked up a plasticine model. It was of a girl with long blond hair, wearing blue trousers and a white top.

'That's Sarah,' she said, holding it out to him. 'That's what she looks like. Well, sort of. It's a bit hard to make a plasticine nose.'

Jack wasn't listening to her. He was staring at the painting set that lay on the carpet, amongst all the other model-making equipment.

'You've got my paints.' Jack felt anger welling up inside him. 'I never said you could use them.'

Annie pouted at him. 'I only borrowed them—'

'You took them from my room, and I've told you to keep out of there!' Jack yelled. He needed one place where he could get right away from Annie and everything she stood for.

Annie's face crumpled. 'I didn't think you'd mind.'

'Well, I do! Now go to bed!' Already feeling guilty, Jack grabbed the paint set, and marched out of the room. He'd overreacted, and he knew it. But he was wound up about his father and anyway, Annie was irritating him with all that made-up rubbish about Sarah Slade from the twenty-fifth century, so it served her right. It didn't really bother her anyway. His sister was as thick-skinned as a herd of elephants. Kicking his bedroom door open, he went in and slammed it shut behind him.

Annie sat in bed, fat tears rolling quietly down her cheeks. She hated it when Jack got angry. However hard she tried, she always seemed to annoy him. She couldn't understand why everything she did irritated him so much. She just couldn't do anything right.

'Jack's horrible,' she sniffed. 'I hate him.'

There was a long pause. Then Annie turned to stare through the dying light at the empty space beside her, her eyes wide and surprised.

'Oh, Sarah,' she said. 'You wouldn't *really* do that to Jack. Would you?'

CHAPTER TWO

'People don't have cars any more in the twenty-fifth century. Well, not cars like ours anyway, because petrol's too expensive and it makes too much pollution, so they all use electric cars now. Sarah says we're stupid to keep on using our cars all the time. She says that people in the twenty-fifth century are much more sensible than we are.'

Jack reached across the kitchen table for the last piece of toast, and seriously considered investing some of his pocket money in a pair of ear-plugs. Annie had been talking her head off about Sarah Slade and life in the twenty-fifth century, ever since they'd got up that morning.

He knew, with a sinking feeling, that this would go on all weekend.

'Mum, can you pass me the butter, please?' he asked loudly, cutting through Annie's explanation of how people in the twenty-fifth century had managed to plug the hole in the ozone layer.

Their mother surfaced from behind the morning newspaper, handed the butter to Jack and then disappeared from view again. Jack picked up his knife, wondering irritably how she could possibly concentrate on reading while Annie was gabbling away right next to her. It was like having breakfast with a mad professor every morning, he thought crossly, cutting off a lump of butter and sliding it onto his toast.

The butter dropped right onto his plate. The toast had vanished.

Jack stared down at his plate, unable to believe his eyes, and Annie giggled.

'Sarah says sorry, but she's hungry.'

'Give that toast back!'

'I can't.' Annie shrugged, her eyes dancing with mischief. 'Sarah's eaten it.'

Jack leaned over, and started moving the packet of cornflakes, the milk bottle and the sugar bowl, trying to find out where Annie had hidden the toast, but it was nowhere to be seen. Red with anger, he turned accusingly to her.

'You've put it in your pocket!'

'No, I haven't.' Giggling, Annie pointed at the dress she was wearing. 'I haven't got any pockets.'

'Well, you're sitting on it then!' Jack roared.

'If I am, are you sure you want it back?' Annie asked cheekily, grinning all over her face.

Jack decided that it wasn't worth fighting over a piece of toast, especially if it meant having to listen to more tales of Sarah Slade. He pushed his chair away from the table and got up. So did Annie. Jack just couldn't help glancing suspiciously down at her chair, to see if she *had* been sitting on the toast, but there was nothing there. He frowned. Where had she put it?

'I told you, Sarah took it,' Annie said, as she noticed him staring at her chair.

'Well, I hope it chokes her,' Jack said shortly. He went out of the kitchen and into the living room. Annie followed him.

'Can I watch *Russian for Beginners*?' she asked, as Jack flicked on the TV.

'No chance.' Jack tuned into one of the music channels, found a noisy rock video and sat back in his chair, clutching the remote control firmly. 'Go away.' And take Sarah Slade with you, he added silently.

Hands on hips, Annie threw him a haughty look. Jack grinned to himself, pleased that he'd got the upper hand for once, and settled down to watch the music video. But the rock band had vanished. Now a man with horn-rimmed glasses and a 1970s pullover filled the screen.

'Da,' he was saying earnestly. 'Oomenya zavoot Ivan.'

'Thanks, Sarah.' Annie grinned triumphantly at Jack. '"Da" – that's Russian for yes. Is he saying "My name is Ivan", Sarah?'

Jack stared at the screen and then at the remote control in his hand. What was going on? Quickly he tapped in the number of the music channel again.

'Repeat after me,' said Seventies man, 'Oomenya zavoot . . .'

'Oomenya zavoot Annie,' said Annie, frowning hard as she concentrated on the screen.

The channel didn't change. Jack tapped in the number of the music channel again and again, but nothing happened. Then he tried all the other stations too. But he couldn't shift *Russian for Beginners*.

'Da,' said the man again, 'Good. Harosho.'

'Does that mean "good", Sarah?' Annie asked calmly. She ignored Jack who was frenziedly shaking the remote control and pressing all the buttons one after the other.

'Desvedanya,' said the man, and the credits started to roll.

'That must be goodbye,' Annie translated. 'Come on, Sarah. Let's go and play upstairs.' She turned away, then glanced back over her shoulder.

'Desvedanya, Jack,' she said with a cheeky grin, as she went out of the living room.

Jack gave the remote control one final, angry shake. Suddenly the rock band were back on screen, and blasting out at full volume. Jack rushed to turn them down, and dropped the remote control on the floor.

'For goodness' sake, Jack!' his mother yelled from the kitchen, 'turn that TV down!'

'There's something wrong with the telly!' Jack yelled back. He launched himself at the floor, grabbed the remote control, and turned the volume off. Then he climbed back into his chair, and tested all the channels, one by one. No problem now. There must have been something temporarily wrong before. Trust Annie to use it for yet another Sarah Slade episode though, Jack thought grimly. As if he was supposed to believe that it was Sarah who'd made the TV go funny like that. Did he look that much of a fool?

Jack settled down again and tried to listen to the music, but he found himself flicking through all the channels one by one, unable to concentrate. He forced himself to focus on what was nagging away at the back of his mind, and re-

38

alized, with a pang, that he was still worrying about his father's phone call. It was all very well deciding not to say anything until his mum had made up her mind what she was going to do, but Jack wasn't sure how much more of this he could take. After all, he'd only heard about his father getting in touch yesterday, and he was already wound up almost to bursting point. How much longer could he go on like this? And what if his mother decided not to tell him after all?

If only there was some way he could force the issue, Jack thought longingly. Maybe his mother wanted to tell him, but she didn't know how to start. He could at least help her along a bit by giving her an opening . . .

He leapt up from the chair as an idea struck him. His saxophone. The saxophone his father had given him. He could get the saxophone out from under his bed, maybe even pretend he'd forgotten it was there, and ask his mum if he could start having lessons. That would be the perfect opportunity to lead the conversation round to his father, if only he could pull it off . . . Eagerly Jack ran out of the room and up the stairs. It was definitely worth a try.

As he went along the landing, he glanced into Annie's room. The door was open, and she was sitting on the floor, surrounded by what looked like a model of an entire space-age town.

Although Jack didn't want to seem interested, he couldn't help stopping and staring. Strange silver buildings, of all shapes and sizes, covered almost the entire space between the bed and the opposite wall. Jack felt himself shiver uneasily, although he didn't know why. He had to force himself to move away before Annie looked up and saw him, and started one of her long, complicated explanations.

Inside his bedroom, Jack lay on the floor, and pushed his hand underneath the bed. With a strange ache right in the centre of his chest, he wondered if his father would remember that he'd given him the saxophone. Over the last few years Jack had sometimes almost hated himself a little for hanging on to it so determinedly. It had somehow seemed to be a sign of weakness. But he hadn't quite been able to make himself get rid of it.

He couldn't feel the saxophone case, so he stretched out a little more, and pushed his hand further underneath. Nothing. Frowning, Jack reached for the torch on his desk and shone the beam of light under the bed.

The saxophone had gone.

Jack stared at the empty space where the saxophone case had been. His heart began to thump wildly. Then he jumped to his feet, and raced out of the bedroom. His mother must have moved it for some reason. That was the only explanation. Annie was banned from his bedroom, and she probably didn't even know the instrument was under the bed, anyway. But as Jack ran past her room, something made him stop and go in.

'Annie!' Jack couldn't get much further than the doorway, because there were too many models on the floor. 'Annie, have you taken my saxophone?'

'No.' Annie was re-modelling Sarah's nose, and didn't look up. But there was something in her voice that didn't sound quite right. Immediately Jack charged into the room, knocking over a couple of skyscrapers covered in tin foil.

'You liar!' he yelled at her. 'What have you done with it?'

Annie looked up at him.

'I haven't got it,' she mumbled. She didn't like it when Jack got angry, but this time it served him right. Sarah had said so.

'Don't give me that!' Furiously Jack started scrabbling through the books and papers on her desk. 'You'd better give it back to me right now or—'

'I said I haven't got it!' Annie retorted more strongly.

Jack spun round and stared at her. 'But you know where it is,' he said, narrowing his eyes.

Annie hesitated. 'Maybe I do,' she said at last.

'So.' Jack took a threatening step towards her. 'Where is it?'

Annie pushed her bottom lip out defiantly. 'Sarah's got it.'

'Sarah?' For a moment Jack had to stop and think who Sarah was. Then, when he realized whom she meant, he almost exploded with fury.

'Sarah? You mean someone who doesn't *exist* has got my saxophone?'

'Sarah's real,' Annie said indignantly.

'Yeah, as real as the Tooth Fairy!' Jack yelled, clenching his fists. Annie gave him a mutinous glare, and he realized, even through the white heat of his rage, that he was going about things the wrong way. Taking a deep, steadying breath, he forced himself to appear calm.

'Annie, could you please ask Sarah to give me my saxophone back?'

Annie shook her head. She wasn't looking at Jack, she was staring over his left shoulder, as if she could see someone behind him.

'What shall I tell him, Sarah?'

'What?' Instinctively Jack swung round to look behind him. There was no-one there. 'Who're you talking to?'

'To Sarah, of course,' Annie said impatiently.

'And she says she won't give you your saxophone back.'

'Why not? Don't tell me, Sarah the time-traveller wants to learn to play the saxophone!' Jack clutched wildly at his forehead. 'Annie, don't do this to me.'

'Sarah says you were horrible to me, and that's why she took your saxophone.' Annie shrugged. 'She says you'd better be nice to me from now on, or you won't get it back. Ever.'

Jack stared at her, open-mouthed. He was beginning to wonder if he was actually asleep, and trapped in some terrible nightmare. If he was, he hoped he'd wake up soon.

'Give me my saxophone back. Now,' he said, shooting the words out from between clenched teeth like bullets.

'I've just told you,' Annie pointed out gently. 'Sarah's got it.'

Then Jack noticed the model of Sarah that Annie was holding. In Sarah's pink plasticine hand was a tiny saxophone, also made of plasticine. That did it. Shaking all over with fury, he launched himself at his sister.

'Where's my saxophone? You'd better give it back right now, or else—'

'I *told* you,' Annie wailed. 'Sarah's got it!'

'Stop saying that!' Jack grabbed the model

of Sarah from Annie, and, with all his strength, crushed it into a multi-coloured ball. Then he flung it down in front of his sister. 'That's what I think of your stupid Sarah!'

Annie took one look at the ruined model, and burst into noisy tears.

'Sarah thinks you're the rudest, nastiest boy she's ever met, and so do I!' she roared.

Breathing hard, Jack stood and glared at her, wondering yet again just what he'd done to deserve a sister like her. Then there was the sound of angry footsteps on the stairs. Seconds later, their mum appeared in the doorway.

'What's going on in here?' she shouted. 'Jack, what have you done?'

CHAPTER THREE

'Jack, I know you want your saxophone back,' his mother said gently, 'but I'm sure that wherever it is, it's quite safe. After all, Annie hasn't been outside this morning, so it must still be in the house.'

'Yes, but where?' Jack muttered. He and his mother had turned the whole place over from top to bottom, and there hadn't been a sniff of the missing saxophone anywhere. Meanwhile Annie was still insisting that Sarah Slade from the twenty-fifth century had taken it to teach Jack a lesson. She'd told their mother that too, even after she had given her a serious talking-to.

'Look, this isn't easy, I know.' His mother sat down on the sofa next to Jack, and put her arm round him. 'But I'm going to ask you to be patient. You know that Annie's having a lot of problems settling into school at the moment . . .'

Jack nodded tightly. He could guess only too well what was coming next.

'And with so much going on . . .' His mum got up and walked nervously round the room. Jack wondered briefly if she was going to tell him now that his father had phoned, but she didn't. 'Well, if this imaginary friend is helping her to cope . . .'

'We should just keep quiet and let her get on with it.' Jack hadn't meant to sound so bitter, but that was how the words came out.

His mother sighed.

'I know it's asking a lot of you, Jack, and I hate having to do it. But Annie's such a handful, and I don't really know how to deal with it . . .' Her voice tailed away, and they sat there in silence for a few seconds.

'You could see if some of those people you contacted could help,' Jack suggested tentatively. His mum had written to several organizations for gifted children, and had got hold of some leaflets, but she'd never done anything else about it. There had to be *somebody* out there who could help them though, Jack thought tensely. At the moment his mum on her

46

own didn't seem to be doing a very good job with Annie, however hard she tried.

'Maybe . . .' But Jack could hear the note of reluctance in his mother's voice. 'I just don't want Annie to feel like a freak. I want her to stay as ordinary as possible. I mean, she's still just a baby.'

A baby with a bigger brain than either of us, Jack thought. But he didn't say it.

They sat in silence again for a few minutes. Jack had to bite down hard on his bottom lip to stop himself from shouting out, 'What about me? Don't I matter too? If Annie wasn't around and having all these problems at school, would you have told me straightaway that dad had phoned? Why is it always Annie, Annie, Annie?' Oh, sure, he understood that Annie was different, and that she had to be treated differently. Even he admitted that. But that didn't stop him from secretly feeling that it just wasn't fair. He was *always* the one who had to give in over *everything*.

'All right,' he said reluctantly. 'I won't mention the saxophone any more. For the moment, anyway.'

His mum gave him a grateful squeeze.

'Thanks, love. And I'm sure it'll turn up safe and sound as soon as Annie gets fed up with Sarah, and starts another game. So,' she forced a bright smile which didn't fool Jack one bit, 'what are you going to do today?'

'Nicko's coming over, and we're going to the park.'

'Oh, Jack, I hate to ask, but would you take Annie with you?' Jack immediately opened his mouth to say no, but his mother rushed on, 'I've got some work to do for Monday, and I won't have time otherwise.'

'All right,' Jack said with a sigh. His mum was a secretary. She was hoping to get promoted soon, so she often did extra work at the weekends.

'Nicko can stay for dinner if you like,' his mother said with a smile. 'Fish and chips OK?'

His favourite. Blackmailed by his own mother.

'Sure.' Jack forced a smile.

'Thanks, love.' His mother went over to the door. 'Annie!' she called up the stairs. 'Come on, sweetheart, Jack and Nicko are going to take you to the park.'

Under protest, Jack added silently. At the moment, he'd rather be as far away from Annie as possible. And from the look Annie gave him when she marched down the stairs and into the living room, it seemed she felt exactly the same way about him. She'd re-made the plasticine model of Sarah, and was holding it tightly in her hand.

'What time's Nicko coming?' their mother asked.

'He said about eleven,' Jack muttered, 'So he should be here any minute.'

'I like Nicko,' Annie announced loudly.

'Meaning what?' Jack shot her a sideways glare.

'Meaning I like Nicko, of course,' Annie said, sticking her tongue out at him.

Jack flicked her another glance, but didn't say anything. Jealousy rushed through him, the kind of jealous, mixed-up feelings he often had when Annie and Nicko were together. But it wasn't his fault that he and Annie didn't get on, was it, he asked himself with silent bitterness. It wasn't as if he didn't want a little sister. He did. But he wanted the kind of little sister he could help and protect; the kind of little sister who didn't know more than he did, so he would be able to teach her all about the world; the kind of little sister who'd look up to him and think he was the best thing since sliced bread. But Annie wasn't like that. She didn't need helping and protecting, she certainly didn't need teaching and there was no way she looked up to him. Was it any wonder that they didn't get on?

'By the way, you two . . .' Their mother was sorting through the muddle of magazines and books on the coffee table, and flinging them haphazardly onto the floor. 'You haven't seen my Filofax, have you? You know, the black diary I use for work? I can't find it anywhere, and I know I left it on this table.'

Jack shook his head.

'I haven't seen it.' Then he looked down, and drew in a sharp breath. 'But maybe you'd better ask Annie.'

'Annie?' Their mum look round. 'Have you seen it, love?'

Annie hesitated. Then slowly she held out the plasticine model of Sarah. Instead of Jack's saxophone, the doll was now holding a tiny black book.

'Sarah's got it,' she muttered.

'Sarah?' Their mother raised her eyebrows.

'Sarah Slade from the twenty-fifth century,' Jack said helpfully. He knew it was nasty, but he couldn't help feeling just a glimmer of satisfaction. Maybe his mum would start taking Annie's game a bit more seriously now.

'Oh.' Jack saw his mother rein in her temper with a superhuman effort, before she came over to Annie and put her hands on her shoulders. 'Sweetheart, I can't get on with my work without that diary. Would you please ask Sarah to give it back?'

Annie turned to the space between herself and Jack, and stood there for a few seconds, nodding her head as if she was listening hard. Instinctively Jack moved away slightly. Of course he knew there wasn't anyone standing next to him, but he couldn't help it.

'Sarah says she won't give it back,' Annie said at last. 'She said you were horrible to me this morning.'

Jack watched his mother take a deep breath.

'Annie, I wasn't "horrible" to you. I was just worried about Jack's saxophone. Now will you please give me my diary back?'

'Sarah says no,' Annie said defiantly.

They all stood there in silence. Then the door-bell rang, making them all jump.

'That'll be Nicko,' Jack said.

'I'll go and get my coat.' Annie turned away, and skipped up the stairs as if she hadn't got a care in the world.

Their mother groaned. 'Oh no! I can't get on with my work without that diary!'

Jack shrugged. At least now his mother knew how annoying it was to be a victim of Sarah Slade the time-traveller.

'That's two things Annie's taken already,' he said as he went over to the door. 'I wonder what she's going to nick next?'

His mother looked upset. 'Don't say that, Jack. Annie's not a thief.'

Maybe not, Jack thought to himself as he went

51

down the hall to let Nicko in. But she certainly wasn't far off. And if 'Sarah' was going to take her 'revenge' on everyone who annoyed Annie, where would it all end?

'Wow!' Nicko said when Jack flung open the front door. 'Who rattled your cage, buster?'

Jack shrugged. 'If you really want to know, a time-traveller nicked my saxophone.'

Nicko grinned.

'Sounds like a headline from a Sunday newspaper. So what's up?'

'I just told you.' Jack turned and shouted up the stairs 'Annie! Get a move on.'

'No, seriously.' Nicko squinted at him.

'Seriously, you remember Sarah Slade from the twenty-fifth century? Well, she's taken my saxophone.' Jack bit the words out through gritted teeth. Despite what he'd said to his mum, he was still seething inside. Annie and her extraordinary abilities had dominated their lives for too long, and he was coming to the end of his patience. 'Or so I've been told.'

Nicko's eyes were as round as marbles.

'Why?'

Jack shrugged. He didn't really want to tell Nicko about the row he'd had with Annie the night before.

'Maybe they don't have saxophones in the twenty-fifth century. Who knows?'

'Outrageous.' Nicko shook his head in disbelief. 'Where does Egghead get these ideas from?'

'Don't ask me, I'm just her brother,' Jack said. 'Is there a swap shop for sisters anywhere?'

'I heard that.' Annie was coming down the stairs behind him. 'Sarah says that if this was the twenty-fifth century, you'd be exiled to the planet Mars.'

'Mars sounds great to me,' Jack muttered. 'Miles away from you and Sarah both.' He turned away to pick up his jacket, missing the hurt look Annie gave him. Nicko saw it, though.

'Is Sarah coming with us to the park?' he asked quickly.

'Of course she is.' Annie pointed at the space next to her. 'She's right here.'

'Oh, good,' said Jack. 'Sure she wouldn't like to make herself visible, so we can all see what an eleven-year-old saxophone thief from the twenty-fifth century looks like?'

'Sarah says, thanks for showing her what an idiot-brained eleven-year-old boy from the 1990s looks like,' Annie retorted quickly. Nicko gave a muffled snort of laughter, which he tried to turn, not very successfully, into a cough. Jack glared at him.

'Come on, let's go.'

'So why can't the rest of us see Sarah?' Nicko

asked curiously as the three of them walked down the street. Jack felt like kicking him. Why couldn't Nicko just keep his big fat mouth shut? he thought angrily. Anyone would think he was really interested.

Annie looked at the empty space next to her, raised her eyebrows and then waited for a few seconds, as if she was listening to someone talking.

'Sarah doesn't want anyone to see her except me,' she said, after a few seconds.

'Why not?' Nicko asked.

'Yeah, why not?' Jack muttered under his breath. 'There are a few things I'd like to say to Sarah Slade. In person.'

Annie ignored him, and looked at Nicko.

'Sarah says it's easier this way.'

Nicko nodded, as if he understood. At least he believed her, Annie thought happily. Nicko didn't seem to mind that she was 'different'; he treated her just the same as he treated everyone else.

'How's Sarah's history project going?' Nicko asked. He sounded genuinely interested too, Jack thought scornfully.

'Really well,' Annie said enthusiastically. 'I've told her lots and lots about the 1990s. And she's told me all about the twenty-fifth century.'

'Like what?'

'Well, she says that people in the twenty-fifth century are much nicer than they are now.'

That was probably another dig at him, Jack thought bitterly, but he kept his mouth shut.

'Sarah says that everyone in the twenty-fifth century would like me because I'm clever,' Annie went on eagerly. 'She says they like clever people there.'

'They must be daft then,' Jack muttered under his breath. Annie's bottom lip trembled at that, but he didn't notice.

As they carried on down the street, Nicko kept glancing nervously at the empty space next to Annie. What was the matter with him? Jack thought furiously. Nicko, the complete dork, was acting as if he truly believed that there was somebody there.

'Stop it!' He nudged Nicko in the ribs with his elbow, and Nicko jumped. 'What's the matter with you?'

'Oh, nothing.' Nicko blushed. 'Maybe you ought to think about making some – er – real friends, Annie. It can't be much fun hanging out with someone who's invisible.'

Annie smiled at him. 'But Sarah's my *best* friend.'

'Your only friend, you mean,' Jack said. For an instant, Annie's face crumpled into a hurt look, and Jack wished he hadn't said it. But only for a second. Then Annie stuck her nose in the air with her most haughty and superior look – the one their mum called her 'Queen Bee' look, and which irritated Jack more than almost anything else she did – and poked her tongue out at him.

'I don't want any other friends. I don't *need* any other friends, now that I've got Sarah.'

'Oh, right, you've got to be pretty desperate to have a best friend who doesn't exist.' Jack couldn't stop the words coming out. He was always telling himself not to get into rows with Annie; she was only a little kid, after all. But the problem was she didn't seem like a little kid, and she wound him up so much, he just couldn't help himself.

'She *does* so exist!' Annie said furiously. 'Nicko believes me!'

'No, he doesn't.' Jack turned to look at his friend. It was definitely time for Nicko to show where his true loyalties lay. 'You don't believe in Sarah Slade from the twenty-fifth century, do you, Nicko?'

'Er – well . . .' Nicko looked uncomfortable. 'Well . . .'

'Come on, Nicko, it's an easy question.' Jack nudged him again. 'Do you believe in Sarah Slade or not?'

Nicko bit his lip. 'Well, no, not really . . .' His voice tailed away.

Annie stared at him with wide, hurt eyes. 'Sarah doesn't like you any more, and neither do I!' she announced loudly. Then she turned and marched off towards the children's playground.

'Come on, Nicko, let's go and play on the rope ladders.' Feeling guilty again, Jack glanced over his shoulder to check that Annie was OK. A strange ache clutched at his chest as he watched her toddling over to the baby swings all by herself, in her blue dress and her little blue boots. She looked so sweet and ordinary. Until she went and opened her mouth.

Nicko was looking worried. 'You shouldn't have made me say that.'

Jack knew he was in the wrong, but it couldn't be helped. Anyway, it was Annie's fault for being so irritating.

'She'll get over it. Come on. Race you to the rope ladders.'

Jack managed to forget about Annie and Sarah for a while. Then, when Nicko flopped down onto the grass for a rest, he reluctantly went over to check on his sister. Annie was in the sandpit, and in the middle of explaining the solar system to an open-mouthed five-year-old. Jack didn't bother interrupting. Instead he left her to it, and went back over to Nicko.

'She's giving that kid a lecture about the solar system,' Jack said, sitting down on the grass next to his friend. 'No wonder she hasn't got any mates. Oh, except the wonderful Sarah Slade from the twenty-fifth century, of course.'

Nicko stretched out, looking up at the sky. 'Yeah, it's a shame really, isn't it? Poor old Annie.'

Jack stared at him, not quite believing his ears. 'Poor old *Annie*?'

'Yeah, having to make up a friend because she hasn't got any, and you two don't get on very well either, so . . .' Nicko began to sense that maybe, just maybe, there was some kind of atmosphere developing, and his voice tailed away. Although Jack had never said anything to him, Nicko knew that the relationship between Jack and his sister was a difficult one. Anyone who was around the two of them for long enough couldn't help but notice. Nicko had sometimes wondered why Jack had never confided in him, and at first he'd thought that maybe the problem was that, as a relatively new friend, Jack just didn't trust him enough. But as he'd got older, Nicko had gradually realized that Jack couldn't really discuss his relationship with Annie with anyone, because the whole thing went too deep. The thought made him extremely uneasy.

'I mean,' he went on hastily, 'poor old you as well for losing your saxophone like that.'

'Well, thanks a lot.' Jack pulled viciously at a tuft of grass. He expected a bit of loyalty from his mates at least, even if he didn't get it from anyone else. 'It's nice to know who my friends are.'

'Oh, come on, Jack.' Nicko punched his arm a bit uncertainly. 'Annie's only a little kid, isn't she? You can't put all the blame on her.'

'Oh, yes, I can,' Jack muttered. But a picture of Annie bursting into tears as he crushed the model of Sarah to pieces jumped into his mind, and suddenly he felt guilty. Why, he didn't know. What did he have to feel guilty about? He hadn't done anything. He was the normal, ordinary one. *He* didn't invent stupid games that made everyone's life a misery. But Nicko's words kept on and on repeating themselves in the back of his mind, 'And you two don't get on very well either, so . . .'

Jack felt really angry with Nicko all of a sudden, and he wasn't quite sure why.

'And, while we're on the subject, will you stop asking her about Sarah all the time? It's really getting on my nerves.'

'Sorry.' Nicko looked injured. 'I was just interested, that's all.'

'Well, stop being interested right now! This whole thing's starting to get well out of hand, and I don't want you encouraging her. Who knows what she might do next?'

'What do you mean?' Nicko stared at him, round-eyed.

'Well, she's already taken my sax, and Mum's Filofax as part of this so-called game,' Jack pointed out. 'What if she starts taking other things? Other people's things?'

'Oh, come on, Jack, Annie's not a thief,' Nicko said, just like their mother had done.

Jack didn't answer, and they sat there in silence for a bit. Across the playground, Annie was digging morosely on her own in the sandpit. The boy she'd been talking to had eventually escaped from her lecture on the solar system, and was now careering around the playground pretending to be Thomas the Tank Engine. Annie watched him with a mystified look on her face. She couldn't understand why none of the children she tried so hard to make friends with were ever interested in the same things that she was.

A wasp flew over her head, buzzed around her for a moment and then settled motionless on the sand. Annie squatted down to look at it more closely, admiring the translucent wings and the thin, striped body. She didn't know much about wasps. Maybe she'd find a book about them in the library next time she went. The only thing she knew about wasps, really, was that nobody liked them. Some people just put up with them buzzing around, others slapped them away or ran off when they came closer. Annie's bottom lip quivered for a moment. She knew exactly how that wasp felt. Still, she had Sarah to talk to now, so she didn't have to bother with other people any more. Feeling more cheerful, she turned to Sarah, and smiled at her.

'Do you have parks in the twenty-fifth century, Sarah?'

Jack stared across the playground at his sister, standing all alone in the sandpit and talking animatedly to someone who wasn't there, and felt a familiar rush of irritation. There were only a few other people in the playground, but already everyone was looking at her. Why couldn't Annie just *try* to make a few friends, he thought angrily. Maybe if she had a couple of mates, it'd take her mind off her daft games once and for all. But she just couldn't be bothered, could she? Oh, no, she had to go around being all superior, and frightening all the other kids off by gabbling on about things they just couldn't understand. Suddenly, with a start, he realized that Nicko was talking to him.

'I – er – I suppose Annie's all right, isn't she?'

Jack's attention snapped abruptly back to what his friend was saying. 'What do you mean?'

'Well,' Nicko concentrated on looking very hard at the grass. 'You know. All right.'

Jack suddenly realized exactly what Nicko meant. 'Are you trying to say my sister's crazy or something?'

'No, not really . . .'

'Well, what then?' Jack's voice was getting louder and louder. He couldn't help it. 'You know what she's like. She's just too brainy, that's all. There's nothing wrong with her.'

'I know that,' Nicko said nervously. 'It's just the way she gets into these games of hers. Especially this one. I mean, she seems to think it's really happening. And it can't be. Can it?'

'What do you mean, can it?' Jack stared at him in amazement. 'You don't believe in Sarah Slade from the twenty-fifth century, do you?'

'Of course I don't.' But Nicko sounded less than sure, and Jack burst out laughing.

'You dummy, you'll be saying you believe in ghosts next!'

Nicko looked embarrassed, and began fiddling with his shoelaces.

'Well, some people do,' he muttered weakly.

'Some people are stupid enough to believe anything.'

'I don't really believe her.' Nicko looked a bit shamefaced. 'But you have to admit she's convincing the way she talks to Sarah. It's just as if she can see and hear someone we can't.'

'Yes, but half the time I'm sure she just does it because she knows it winds me up,' Jack muttered, digging his heels into the turf. 'And she's so good at it, you can't tell when she's doing it either.'

'Why would Annie want to wind you up?' Nicko asked cautiously. He was always giving Jack an opportunity to start talking about Annie, if he wanted to. Jack never did, but Nicko never stopped giving him the chance either.

'Well . . .' Jack stared down at the grass, and cleared his throat. 'You know what brothers and sisters are like,' he finished lamely.

It was much, much more than that, but he couldn't say so, not even to Nicko. He'd never admitted just how much he secretly resented Annie even to himself, let alone to anybody else. Quickly he stood up, putting an end to the dangerous conversation.

'Come on. I said we'd get back by one.'

They collected Annie, and were on their way back to the gates, when Nicko suddenly stopped dead in the middle of the path with an exclamation of horror.

'Look out,' Annie said. 'Sarah almost walked straight into you.'

Jack ignored her, and looked at Nicko.

'What's up?'

Nicko was frantically slapping his jacket pockets. 'I don't believe it. I think I've lost my glasses.'

'What, again?' Jack shook his head. 'I thought you'd got a new pair.'

'I have. Had.' Nicko started going through the pockets of his jeans. 'My mum bought me some gold-framed ones last week. That's the fourth pair I've had in the last six months.'

'You ought to put them on,' Jack said. 'At least then you'd know where they were.'

Nicko was still frantically rooting through his pockets without success.

'My mum's going to hang me out to dry,' he groaned. 'She said if I lost these, she was going to Sellotape the next pair to my ears.'

'Great fashion statement,' Jack remarked. 'You might start a trend.'

'Sorry to be a pain, but can we go back and look?' Nicko pulled a face. 'They might've fallen out of my pocket when I took my jacket off.'

'OK.' Jack glanced over at Annie. 'Come on, we'll all go and look.'

Annie avoided Jack's gaze, and didn't say anything. Jack stared hard at her, and all of a sudden, a cold finger of ice slid down his spine. Don't be an idiot, he told himself sharply. Annie wouldn't do something like that. Not to Nicko.

They searched all round the playground, and under the bench where Jack and Nicko had left their jackets, but there was no sign of the glasses anywhere. Jack kept glancing at Annie, and she kept looking back at him with a wide-eyed, innocent stare. But the more Jack thought about it, the more he couldn't help wondering. Annie had been upset when Nicko had said that he didn't believe in Sarah Slade. Had Annie stolen his glasses to teach him a lesson, just like she'd done with Mum's Filofax and Jack's saxophone?

Eventually they gave up, and left. Nobody said anything on the way home. Nicko was too depressed about losing his glasses, Annie was uncharacteristically silent and Jack was thinking furiously. He was trying to remember if Annie had been anywhere near the bench while he and Nicko were playing on the rope ladders. As far as he could remember, she hadn't. But he wasn't sure.

By the time they got home, Nicko had cheered up a bit at the prospect of fish and chips. He and Jack went upstairs to watch TV, and Annie disappeared into her own room straightaway, and shut the door. Nicko put their favourite cartoons on, but Jack couldn't concentrate. All he could think about was Annie, and those glasses. Was his sister really a thief? Just how far would she go to make this stupid – and dangerous – game with her imaginary friend come true?

When Mrs Robinson called up that lunch was ready, Nicko and Jack went out onto the landing, and met Annie coming out of her bedroom. Jack stared at her suspiciously, and she gave him an enigmatic look.

'I'll race you to those fish and chips, kid,' Nicko said to her in a terrible American accent. But Annie ignored him, and went downstairs with her nose in the air.

'Hmm, I don't think I'm too popular at the moment.' Nicko pulled a face. 'How long do you think she'll stay mad at me?'

'Who knows?' His heart pounding wildly, Jack waited for Nicko to make the connection between Annie being annoyed and his missing glasses, but he didn't seem to realize.

'Come on then, get a move on.' Nicko slapped Jack on the back, and headed down the stairs himself. 'I'm starving.'

'You go down, I'm going to the loo,' Jack called after him. 'Tell my mum I'll only be a minute.'

He turned to go to the bathroom, then stopped. The door to Annie's room was open. Hesitating only for a second, Jack moved silently across the landing, and slipped inside. Side-stepping the tall, silver buildings, he went straight over to the model of Sarah Slade. He could see it lying on the desk. The plasticine models of his saxophone and his mum's diary were next to it, and in Sarah's hand now was a tiny pair of gold-framed glasses, made from a twisted paperclip.

CHAPTER FOUR

'Something on your mind?' Nicko asked with a frown when he'd beaten Jack at *Mutant Avengers from Planet Poison* five times in a row.

'No.' Jack turned the computer off, and forced a smile. The last thing he wanted was for Nicko to guess what had happened. In fact, he was surprised that Nicko hadn't sussed it already.

'It's just that you thrash me every time, and today you didn't even get past the vat of boiling cyanide,' Nicko observed mildly.

'Sorry?' Jack wasn't listening. He was too busy wondering if Annie was really a thief or not. All he wanted to do was to get rid of Nicko – fast – so he could find out. 'Look, I'll see you tomorrow morning as usual, all right?'

'Fine.' Nicko said, looking a bit surprised. He got to his feet, and picked up his jacket. 'See you tomorrow then.'

Jack heard his footsteps clattering down the stairs, and then the sound of the front door opening and closing. He breathed a sigh of relief, slumped down onto his bed, and buried his head in the pillow. Not only had he lost his saxophone, he might also be on the way to losing his best friend. Nicko wouldn't be too pleased when he knew it was Jack's sister who'd taken his glasses and got him into serious grief with his mum. And even if Jack didn't tell him, Nicko was bound to realize sooner or later.

Jack punched his pillow a few times in frustration. He felt as if his life would never be right again. It was a feeling he'd had ever since his father had left, but now things were getting out of control. There was no doubt about it; Annie had to be stopped. He would have to tell his mother that he suspected his sister was a thief. Surely then his mum would *do* something? She'd have to, even if it meant calling in some outside help.

Jack felt an intense determination to put his life to rights, and deal with Annie once and for all. He jumped off his bed, ran out onto the landing and leaned over the banisters.

'Mum?' he called down the stairs. 'I need to talk to you. It's important.'

'Can it wait a couple of minutes?' His mother was standing by the back door. 'I just need to have a quick word with Lucy.'

'All right.'

Jack waited until his mum had gone out into the back garden. Then he went across the landing to Annie's room. While his mother was talking to their neighbour, this was his chance to get at Annie, and make her confess. Maybe if he could get the glasses back before Nicko realized what had happened, he could give them back, and pretend he'd dropped them in their house or something. And if he could get the glasses back before he went to his mother, it would prove to her that Annie was going to get into serious trouble if she kept on like this. One way or another, it was time this Sarah Slade game was sorted out. Sorted out and stopped.

He knocked on Annie's door.

'Annie?'

'Go away. I'm busy.'

It wasn't a good start. But Jack opened the door and went in, anyway. Annie was sitting on the window sill, drawing in a large notebook. She glared at him.

'I said I was busy.'

'I know. But this won't take long.' This time,

Jack intended to stay cool. This time, he was going to remain calm, whatever Annie said about Sarah Slade. 'Can I sit next to you?'

Annie shook her head.

'Sarah's sitting there.'

'Oh.' Jack's resolve to keep his cool was already being severely tested. Taking a deep breath, he knelt down on the carpet in front of his sister, so that his face was level with hers. 'I want to talk to you.'

'Why?' Annie looked suspicious. 'You *never* want to talk to me.'

Jack swallowed an angry retort. 'Don't be silly. Of course I do.'

Annie stared intently at the empty space on the window sill next to her. 'Sarah says if you're being nice, you must want something.'

Jack bit his tongue, and counted to ten. 'Maybe Sarah could go outside and wait on the landing,' he said. 'I want to talk to you privately.'

Annie shook her head.

'Sarah says no way. She says you're being too nice by half, and she wants to stay and find out what's going on.'

Jack hung on to the remaining shreds of his cool with difficulty. He was coming very close indeed to aiming a punch at thin air.

'All right.' He stared Annie straight in the eye.

He tried not to look at the empty space next to her, but the hairs on the back of his neck were prickling. It was almost as if there was somebody else in the room, watching him. He knew it was stupid, but it was a measure of just how powerful Annie's games could be.

'Tell me the truth, Annie –' he fixed her with a solemn stare '– did you take Nicko's. glasses when we were at the park?'

'No,' Annie said, so definitely that Jack believed her. Until she said, 'Sarah did.'

Jack's last reserves of cool collapsed completely.

'ANNIE!' he roared, banging his fist down on her desk, and almost flattening his knuckles in the process. 'Stop this right now!'

'Stop what?' Annie looked innocently at him.

'All this stuff about Sarah.' Jack grabbed her shoulders and shook her. 'Sarah isn't real, and she didn't take Nicko's glasses.'

'Yes, she did,' Annie retorted, pulling away from him.

'She didn't!'

'She did!'

'She didn't!' Jack fought for control, and tried desperately to regain the upper hand. 'You took them, didn't you?'

'No!' Annie was so outraged, Jack almost believed her again. Almost. 'Sarah did. She said

72

Nicko was horrible to me, and she was going to teach him a lesson.'

'Sarah doesn't exist! You took them, and I'm going to tell Mum!' Jack yelled. 'Listen to me, Annie! You can't just go round nicking other people's things just because they've annoyed you!'

'I didn't take anything!' Annie said indignantly. 'Anyway, Sarah said it served Nicko right. He pretended he believed me, and he didn't really.'

Jack gritted his teeth.

'Can you blame him?' he shouted at her. 'You're saying you've got an invisible friend from the twenty-fifth century who goes around stealing from people who annoy you, to teach them a lesson, and we're expected to believe you! Come off it, Annie! We all know it's you!'

Annie glanced across at 'Sarah', as if she was listening to her, and then looked back at her brother. 'Prove it,' she said with a little smile.

Jack blinked. 'What?'

'Sarah said, prove it.' Annie shrugged her shoulders. 'I didn't take Nicko's glasses, and you can't prove that I did.'

Jack opened his mouth to object. Then, with a sickening jolt, he realized that she was right. For all he knew, Nicko could have lost his glasses accidentally, and Annie could just be using it as

73

part of her game. After all, he hadn't actually seen her take them, and neither had Nicko. Anger fired through him. He couldn't prove it, even though he truly believed that Annie had taken them. So his only chance of getting Nicko's glasses back was by getting her to confess. Forcing himself to hold back, he thought hard. Arguing like this wasn't getting him anywhere. He had to try something different.

'Annie,' he said in a calmer voice, 'do you really think Sarah's your friend?'

Annie gave him a surprised look. 'Of course she is.'

'Is she?' Jack fixed his eyes on her. 'Think about it. All she's done so far is to get you into trouble.'

Annie shook her head vigorously. 'No, she hasn't. Sarah sticks up for me when everyone else is being horrible.'

'No, she doesn't, she gets you into trouble,' Jack persisted. '*She* takes things, and *you* get blamed for it.'

Annie glanced uncertainly across at 'Sarah', and Jack felt an icy shiver unexpectedly ripple down his spine. He had to agree with Nicko that it was frightening the way Annie seemed to be able to see someone no-one else could. Her act was utterly convincing.

74

'Sarah says it's not our fault.' Annie looked defiantly at Jack. 'If everyone believed me, it would be all right.'

Jack tried hard to hold onto his calm demeanour, but he could feel it slipping away like a landslide. 'Why should we believe you, Annie? I mean, we can't see Sarah, can we?'

'But she's here!' Annie seemed close to tears now. 'She really is! And I don't tell lies. I don't!'

Jack stared at her uncertainly. It was true that Annie never told lies. She was completely and totally honest, mainly because she was so obsessed with facts. And never before had she claimed that any of her other games were as real as this one. But that didn't make Jack believe in Sarah Slade. On the contrary, it just made him more and more convinced that Annie was doing it to wind him, and everyone else, up. That made him really mad. The alternative, which was unthinkable, was that her mind was somehow disturbed, and his thoughts flashed briefly back to his conversation with Nicko earlier that day.

'Annie, listen to me—' he said desperately.

Downstairs the telephone started to ring. Jack waited for his mother to answer it, then remembered that she wasn't there. He made for the door, leaping over a couple of silver-domed buildings on the way.

'I haven't finished with you yet,' he warned

Annie as he went out onto the landing. 'I'm going to tell Mum exactly what's going on.'

Annie threw him a look of dislike that hit him right between the eyes. 'Tell her if you want to,' she snapped. 'But Sarah won't like it.'

Then she swung the door shut behind him.

Jack ran down the stairs, cursing Annie, Sarah Slade and everybody in the twenty-fifth century. He skidded on the last step, hurled himself down the hall and grabbed the receiver.

'Hello?'

There was a long pause. Maybe it was Sarah Slade ringing to confess that she'd stolen Nicko's glasses was one of the thoughts that passed wildly through his mind. Then, at last, someone spoke.

'Jack?'

Jack couldn't speak. There was another long, long pause. And then Jack said, 'Dad?', just as in America his father said, 'Jack?' again.

There was another agonizing silence. Then Jack managed to get out, 'Yes, it's me.'

'How are you, son?'

'Fine.'

Jack felt as if all the gravity had suddenly disappeared from the atmosphere, and he was like an astronaut who had to do everything in slow motion. He moved slowly and painfully across to sit on the bottom stair, feeling as if he was pushing his way through thick treacle.

'Good.' Because of the time delay, there were strange, lengthy pauses between everything they were saying, and his father's voice sounded echo-ey and far away, as if he was speaking through a long tube. 'How's your mum? Did she tell you I'd phoned?'

'Yes, she did.' It was a lie, but it was easier than going into long, complicated explanations.

'Oh, good.' His father sounded relieved. His voice was familiar, and yet, in a curious way unfamiliar too because of the thin overlay of an American accent. 'How's Annie?'

'Fine.'

Another long pause stretched away over the Atlantic Ocean.

'Um – I guess you want to know why I haven't been in touch . . .' His father's voice tailed away, and for a second Jack thought they'd been cut off.

'I suppose so,' he muttered, marvelling that his own voice could sound so cold and hard and bitter. He wondered if it would still sound like that after travelling thousands and thousands of miles along a telephone cable. He thought it probably did, because his father's next words sounded even more strained.

'Sorry, Jack. It was just that – well, I had a bit of a rough time when I first got over here . . .'

'Yes, you must have done. If you couldn't afford to write a letter or make a phone call.' Jack was amazed by his own ability to sound calm and cool and collected while his insides were churning round and round like a washing machine. 'Things must have been really tough.'

There was another echo-ey pause.

'All right, I guess I deserved that,' said his father with a sigh. 'To cut a long story short, the sax job I had lined up when I first came over fell through, and I've been – well, not exactly homeless, but not far off. Anyway, I've got a regular job in a jazz band now, so things are a lot better.'

'That's lucky, because this call must be costing you a fortune.' Jack hadn't meant to sound sarcastic but he did. The question he wanted to ask most of all was if his father was coming back to England, but he would have died before he let those words out of his mouth.

'Annie must be pretty big by now.'

'She's five,' Jack said shortly. His dad could count, couldn't he? Or had he forgotten Jack's age too?

'Yes, of course she is . . .' During the next awkward silence, Jack tried to picture his father at the other end of the line. What did he look like? It was getting increasingly hard to remember without the help of a photograph.

'Did she turn out pretty bright?' his dad was

saying, 'I remember what she was like before I—'

He stopped and the atmosphere between them thickened with unspoken guilt.

'Yes,' Jack said, 'she's bright.' King of the understatement, that's me, he thought grimly.

The back door opened suddenly, and Jack gave a guilty start.

'Jack?' His mother came down the hallway. 'Who's that on the phone?'

Jack didn't say a word, but he didn't have to. The look on his face gave him away. His mother turned white, and held out her hand for the receiver. Mutely Jack handed it over, wishing he'd been nicer to his father, wanting to say something more, but not knowing what.

'It's me,' his mother snapped into the phone. 'What do you think you're doing? I told you only to ring me at work.'

Jack heard his father start to protest, although he couldn't hear what he was saying.

'What do you mean, you lost the number? That's just so typical of you, Mark! Look, hold on for a minute.'

His mother clapped her hand over the receiver, and gave Jack one of those looks he knew he couldn't argue with.

'Jack, go to your room, please. And close the door.'

Jack went without protest. But he didn't go

into his bedroom. He slammed the door shut while he was still out on the landing, then he crept over to the banisters, and knelt down out of sight, so that he could hear what his mother was saying.

'. . . after all this time, don't you think it's unsettling for the kids? No, I don't think this is the time or the place either.'

There was a long pause then. Up on the landing, Jack could almost hear his mother spitting fire down the receiver.

'You've got to be joking, Mark.' She lowered her voice then, and Jack had to lean right over the banisters to catch what she was saying. 'I wouldn't dream of it. What about school? No, you can forget that right now, and don't go putting any ideas into Jack's head, because it's just not on, all right? I don't care if you're going to pay for the tickets, and I'll believe that when I see them. This is typical of you, thoughtless and inconsiderate. Look, I just can't discuss this with you now.'

Jack's heart started thumping with crazy excitement. His father wanted him to go to America to visit him! He could hardly believe it. It was wonderful; the best thing that had happened to him for a long, long time. Not only that, it would be a chance to get away from Annie and her stupid games for a while. Speaking to his father again had made Jack realize that he still loved him, and he still wanted to see him. He didn't care what his mum said.

Jack was so excited, he hardly listened to any more of the conversation. Anyway, it was all the same stuff he vaguely remembered from when his dad was at home: 'you're so irresponsible', 'you don't think before you speak', etc. etc. When his mother finally banged down the receiver, Jack raced downstairs, caught his foot in the mat at the bottom and crash-landed in the hall.

'Dad wants me to go and visit him in the States?' he gasped breathlessly, not caring that she'd know he'd been listening on the landing. 'Can I go, Mum? Please?'

His mother looked shocked.

'Jack, I told you to go to your room. I didn't want you to find out your dad had been in touch again out of the blue like this.'

'I already knew, I heard you talking to Daniels,' Jack gabbled, not caring now about anything except seeing his father. 'Please, Mum!' He grabbed her hand. 'I can go, can't I?'

'Jack, stop it.' His mother took him gently by the shoulders. 'This is something we need to talk about. Not about a trip to America, that's not going to happen. We have to take time to sort out how we feel about your father coming back into our lives after all this time.'

'I know how I feel!' Jack tore himself away from her, clenching his fists with frustration. 'I want to go and see him!'

'No. Jack, listen to me, please,' his mother said firmly. 'It's not possible. You'd have to have far too much time off school, and anyway, I've got my hands full with Annie at the moment. You know the problems she's been having. I couldn't unsettle her even more by taking her away in the middle of term.'

Jack's heart dropped like a stone.

'I thought Dad wanted me to go over on my own.'

His mother shook her head.

'No, he wants to see both of you. That means I'd have to go as well. It's all too difficult.'

'I could go over on my own,' Jack argued breathlessly.

'No,' his mother said definitely, and Jack knew she was thinking about stories in the newspapers, where parents who lived abroad had kept their children, and wouldn't send them back to Britain. 'If we went – and we're not going – we'd all go together.'

'Well, if we can't go now, can we go over in the Christmas holidays when we won't miss any school?' Jack pleaded.

'No, sweetheart, I'm afraid not. Your dad's going off on tour with his band in seven weeks' time, and he'll be away right through until next April. Typical of him to leave it all till the last minute . . .'

'So it's because of Annie we're not going,' Jack said in a dull voice.

'That's only one of the reasons, Jack. I don't really want you to miss any school either. And I have to say, I'm not very happy myself about the prospect of spending two weeks with your father. Look, I know it's hard for you, love. I know how much you want to see your dad . . .'

His mother gave him a sympathetic look, and put her arms out to him. Jack avoided her. He was trembling all over with pent-up emotion.

'Why does everything always have to suit Annie?' he asked in a voice that shook.

'Jack, I told you. Annie isn't the only reason—'

'She is! I could easily miss two weeks of school. And you and Dad would get on all right, I know you would.' Jack knew this was difficult for his mother too, but it was hard for him to feel much sympathy for her right now. After all, his father was his father because she'd married him. Just because the two of them didn't get on now, that wasn't Jack's fault, was it? He was entitled to see his father if he wanted to. 'Annie's the real reason we're not going!'

His mother looked away.

'Well, all right. She is. But that doesn't alter the fact that it isn't going to happen.'

'What about me? Don't I get a say in anything?'

'Of course you do.'

'No, I don't. It's not fair!' Jack knew that was a cliché coming from an eleven-year-old, but this time he really meant it. 'It's always Annie, Annie, Annie! I never get anything I want!'

His mother looked upset.

'Jack, that's not true.'

'I hate her!' Up on the landing Jack thought he heard Annie's bedroom door open, but he didn't care. He was almost beside himself with misery and anger. He wanted to go and see his dad, and nothing was going to stop him. 'I hate everything!'

'Jack, please.' His mother put her arm around Jack, pulled him into the living room and closed the door. Jack knew it was so that Annie didn't hear what they were saying, and that made him even angrier. 'I'm sorry, sweetheart. I know I'm asking a lot of you.'

'It's all right,' Jack muttered, fighting to get his emotions back under control. He was already feeling ashamed of his outburst. He was used to keeping how he really felt about Annie well out of sight, not just because he didn't want to upset his mum, but because he was a bit ashamed of it himself. After all, although Annie was a pain in the neck and an egghead, she *was* only a little kid, and she *was* his sister. But now his feelings had been churned about so much, he felt a bit like a bottle of fizzy drink that had been shaken up, and was about to pop its top right off. The sheer force of his emotion, the fact that for a few minutes he hadn't been able to control it, was scaring him.

'Sorry,' he said quickly. 'I didn't mean it.'

'No, you're right.' His mother was walking nervously up and down the room. She was looking shell-shocked, as if Jack had frightened her with the force of his feelings, as well as himself. 'I know I spend too much time and energy on Annie, and too little on you. I don't think I've been very fair to you, especially over the last few weeks . . .'

Jack began to see a glimmer of hope, and held his breath.

'Maybe a holiday might be a good idea,' his mum said thoughtfully, 'And half-term's coming up quite soon so you'd only have to miss a week or so of school. And I suppose Annie deserves a chance to get to know her dad again. She hardly remembers him.'

Jack didn't dare say anything, in case he broke the spell. It was as if he'd been granted his heart's desire by a good fairy, and miraculously, it was all coming true.

'Well, why not?' His mother forced a smile. 'I've never been to America, and I've always wanted to go.'

Jack's face lit up.

'Do you mean it?'

'Jack . . .' His mum hesitated, then sighed as his face fell. 'Well, all right then . . .'

'Yes!' Jack punched the air with excitement.

'As long as Annie is comfortable with the idea,' his mother broke in quickly. She frowned. 'I'm not quite sure how she'll take it. After all, she doesn't remember your dad much at all.'

Who cares, Jack thought triumphantly. For once, things were going to be organized to suit him, not Annie.

'Jack, I hate to say this.' His mother's face was strained. 'But if Annie really can't handle this, we'll have to cancel the trip. I promise you faithfully we'll go later on, as soon as we can, but if the idea of this trip makes her problems at school worse, we might have to pull out at the last minute.'

Jack chewed at his lip. So he wasn't quite home and dry yet. But he was going to make sure nothing happened to stop that trip if it killed him.

'Thanks, Mum.'

He went over, and gave her a hug. His mum hugged him back, then she pulled away and put her hands on his shoulders.

'Jack, about you and Annie . . .'

'What about us?' Jack turned quickly away. He didn't want to discuss it. He and Annie had nothing in common, she made his life a total misery and most of the time he didn't even feel as if they were related. He didn't really hate her, but he didn't like her that much either. He thought that was about the best he could say.

His mother stopped for a second, as if she was trying to feel her way.

'I just wish—' she stopped again. 'I just wish you two got on a little better, that's all. I know it's difficult for you, with her being the way she is . . .'

'We get on fine.' Jack picked up the TV remote control, and began studying it intently. There were some things it was just better not to talk about. After all, they all had to live in the same house, and they had to share each others' lives whether they liked it or not, so what was the point in stirring everything up? He turned away, and switched on the TV. His mother sighed, but she was obviously relieved to abandon the conversation herself.

'Well, I'd better go and talk to Annie then. Find out how she feels about the idea before I ring your father back.' She went slowly over to the door. Jack could see that she was dreading it. No-one could ever predict exactly how Annie would react to anything. 'And, Jack, don't be too disappointed if – well, you know.'

She went out. Jack sat and watched TV, but when he thought about it afterwards, he couldn't remember what he'd seen. A few minutes later, he heard his mother's footsteps coming back down the stairs. His heart lurched.

The door opened. Jack could hardly bring himself to look up at her face, but when he did, he saw that she looked puzzled.

'I've talked to Annie. She seems happy enough.'

Jack stared at her.

'You mean she wants to go?'

'She says so.' His mother frowned. 'I tried to talk to her about your dad, but she didn't seem interested. After she'd spent a minute or two discussing it with Sarah, she just said that the trip was fine with her.'

Jack wanted to feel glad. He *was* glad, but underlying it, there was something else. He felt nervous. He felt – what was the word? Spooked.

'She discussed the trip with Sarah?'

'Yes. I'm beginning to think that maybe Sarah's not such a bad influence after all.' His mother smiled at him. 'Having an imaginary friend to talk to seems to be giving Annie the chance to sort out how she feels about things. So it looks like we're definitely going, if your dad really wants us to.' She sighed. Jack felt a bit guilty, but he fought down the impulse to say anything. Nothing was going to stop him from making this trip. Not his mother. Not Annie. Nothing.

'I'd better start making a list.' His mother picked up a notepad from the table, and began hunting round for a pen. 'There's the passports to organize for a start, and we haven't got long, only three weeks or so. I'll let your dad know straightaway, and I'll ring the school first thing on Monday, and tell them.'

She wrote a few things down, and then looked up at Jack.

'So, what did you want to tell me?'

'What?' Jack stared at her blankly.

'You said you had something to tell me. Something important.'

'Oh, that.' Jack remembered Annie and Nicko's glasses, and felt himself turn extremely pale. 'Oh, it wasn't anything . . .'

Well, he couldn't tell his mother now, could he. If he did, if she knew how much the Sarah Slade game was taking over Annie's life and the sort of things it was making her do, she'd cancel that trip to see his dad straightaway. Taking things that belonged to Jack and his mum was one thing. Taking things that belonged to people outside the family, even if it was someone they were close to like Nicko, was quite another.

So he wouldn't tell her. He would do whatever he had to do over the next three weeks, to make sure that Annie (and Sarah Slade) behaved themselves, because nothing was going to stop him from making that trip to America to see his father.

Nothing at all.

CHAPTER FIVE

'Is this true?'

Nicko was waving the note that Jack had passed him during silent reading time. Jack nodded, trying to dodge the tidal wave of children sweeping remorselessly towards the classroom door like a plague of locusts. It was three fifteen, and the home bell had just rung.

Nicko shook his head, and looked bewildered.

'Why did she do it?'

Jack shrugged.

'Wait till we get outside,' he hissed, with a warning glance at their teacher, Mrs Reeves, who was tidying the Maths cupboard not far away.

'Make way for the King.' Bonehead Griffiths strutted up behind Nicko, and gave him a shove that sent him spinning out of the way like a top.

'Oi!' Nicko yelped. 'Watch where you're going!'

Mrs Reeves turned round.

'Are you behaving yourself, Basil?' she enquired suspiciously.

'Yes, miss,' Bonehead said smartly, and sauntered out of the classroom, grinning.

Jack made a face at Bonehead's back. 'He gets worse every day.'

'Never mind Bonehead.' Nicko grabbed Jack's sleeve, and pulled him out into the corridor. 'Did Annie really take my glasses?'

'Yes.' Jack had passed Nicko the note about Annie and his glasses during silent reading time so that Nicko couldn't say or do anything about it right away. No-one spoke at silent reading time unless they had a death wish. Mrs Reeves saw to that. But even so, after Nicko had read the note, Jack had seen his face quietly turn various shades of red and white, as if somebody was experimenting with the colour control on a TV set.

'I suppose it was because I annoyed her,' Nicko said slowly as they went out into the playground. He frowned. 'She took them on Saturday. It's Wednesday now. Why didn't you tell me before?'

Jack shrugged. He hadn't been sure whether to tell Nicko or not. After thinking things over for a few days, he'd wondered if it would be best to leave things alone. Since Nicko's glasses had disappeared four days ago, nothing else had happened. Annie was still involved with Sarah, but neither Jack or his mother had lost any more of their belongings. Their mother had asked Annie not to talk to Sarah at school, and, much to Jack's relief, Annie had agreed. The whole situation seemed to have stabilized. But Jack was still wary. There were two and a half weeks to go before their trip, and he had enough experience of Annie to know just how unpredictable she could be.

'I wasn't sure she'd taken them. Then I thought maybe I could keep it quiet, and just get the glasses back for you. But now . . .' He stopped. 'I need you to help me.'

'Help you do what?'

'You know I told you on Monday that we're going to America to see my dad?'

'Yeah, lucky thing.'

'What I didn't tell you was that we're only going if Annie doesn't get into any more trouble.' Jack sat down on the wall. 'That's why I need you to help me.'

Nicko turned pale. 'What do you think she might do?'

'I don't know,' Jack said. 'That's the problem. All I know is that she's still playing the Sarah Slade game, and that could mean trouble.'

Nicko looked nervously round him and slid along the wall closer to Jack, even though there was hardly anyone else left in the playground by now.

'This is heavy stuff,' he said. 'Don't you think—'

He stopped, as Mr Daniels rounded the corner of the school. His gaze locked onto their bent heads and conspiratorial manner immediately.

'Come along, boys. It's time you were heading off home.'

'We're waiting for my sister, sir,' Jack said, trying to look innocent and knowing he was failing miserably. 'Her class hasn't come out yet.'

Mr Daniels treated them to his 'whatever you're thinking of trying – don't' look, and went off across the playground.

Nicko let out a sigh of relief. 'I bet he thinks we're plotting to torch the school or something.'

'And instead we're trying to stop a five-year-old girl and her imaginary friend from ruining my life.' It sounded almost funny put that way, but it wasn't funny when you were caught in the middle of it, as Jack was. He could feel the tension in him right through to his bones.

'What I was going to say before Daniels so rudely interrupted us,' Nicko went on, 'was that I think you ought to tell your mum.'

'Tell her what?'

'Well, about my glasses, for one thing.'

'Fine. And where does that leave me?' Jack got off the wall, and kicked it instead. 'Me stuck here, and my dad in America, and no chance of seeing him. No way.'

'So where do I come in?'

'I need you to help me keep an eye on Annie.' Jack looked pleadingly at Nicko. 'I want to make sure she doesn't do anything to make my mum cancel the trip.'

Nicko raised his eyebrows. 'Ask me to do something difficult, why don't you.'

'Thanks.' Jack had taken it for granted that Nicko would help him, and he knew he would, whatever objections he raised. 'Mum's told her not to talk to Sarah at school, and she seems to be sticking to that.'

'We'd better synchronize our watches then.' Nicko was being flippant, but Jack could tell that he was still uneasy. He didn't mind that. He didn't exactly feel all that comfortable about it himself. 'Your mission is to take on and defeat a five-year-old girl and a time-traveller from the future. This tape will self-destruct in—'

Jack nudged him in the ribs. 'There's Annie.'

The Reception class were streaming out of the infants' end of the school, clutching large pieces of artwork that flapped in the wind. Annie usually wandered out on her own, but today Jack was surprised to see that she was right in the middle of a group of children. He could also see, even from a distance, that some of the children were actually talking to her. Hope surged through him. Maybe Annie was starting to make friends at last. Secretly, he was convinced that was the only way they were going to get rid of Sarah Slade. Feeling suddenly very cheerful indeed, he elbowed Nicko again.

'Look. I think Annie's finally made some friends.'

Nicko looked, then looked again, more closely than Jack had done. He frowned. The other children weren't talking to Annie. They were saying things to her, but Annie wasn't answering them, and her face looked pinched and white. As Nicko and Jack went across the playground towards them, the children scattered, leaving Annie alone with a large, detailed drawing of a wasp clutched in her hand.

'Hello, Annie,' Jack said cheerfully. 'Are those your new friends?'

'No,' Annie said curtly, walking away.

'But you were talking to them,' Jack persisted,

hurrying after her with Nicko at his heels. 'I saw you.'

'No, I wasn't.' Annie increased her pace.

'Yes, you were.' Jack tried not to sound irritated, even though he was.

'No, I wasn't. They were talking to me, but I wasn't talking to them. I don't like them. They're silly.' Annie gave a superior sniff. Then she crooked one of her arms out, and tilted it as if she was linking arms with someone who wasn't there. The action was so realistic, and looked so natural, that both Jack and Nicko took a nervous step backwards. Jack accidentally trod heavily on Nicko's toes, and Nicko staggered, and let out a yelp. Annie began to giggle.

'Sarah says you two are a real comedy act.' She turned away, her arm still held out. 'Come on, Sarah, let's go home.'

'I don't know how much more of this I can take,' Jack muttered. 'Those kids were actually talking to her. Why didn't she talk back to them, instead of to that blasted Sarah Slade?'

'They weren't talking to her,' Nicko said. 'Didn't you see? They were teasing her.'

'Teasing her?'

'You saw how they took off when we went over. They were having a go at her.'

Jack's face changed. He sprinted forward,

and grabbed Annie's arm from its invisible lock.

'Annie, have you been talking to Sarah in class?'

'Ow, that hurt.' Annie rubbed her arm dramatically. 'You hurt Sarah too.'

Jack gave her a little shake. 'Have you been talking to Sarah in class, when Mum told you not to?'

'I couldn't help it,' Annie returned with dignity. 'Sarah kept on talking to me, so I had to talk back. I tried not to, really I did, but who else am I going to talk to? I only do it quietly when none of the teachers are around. Anyway, Miss Turner doesn't take any notice. She doesn't bother with me much.'

'But some of the other kids in the class must hear you. Were they teasing you about Sarah just now?'

Annie shrugged, and didn't answer. She simply hooked her arm back into Sarah's invisible one, and skipped off down the street towards their house.

Jack groaned.

'That's all we need. Everyone at school's going to know about Sarah Slade by tomorrow.'

'You'd better tell your mum,' Nicko said sensibly.

'No.' Jack was shaking his head before Nicko had finished the sentence. He didn't want his mother to know just how deeply Annie was becoming involved in the Sarah game. If Annie, who was usually reasonably well-behaved, was defying their mother and talking to Sarah in class, their mum was bound to be worried. That could spell disaster for the trip to see his dad. 'We're just going to have to try and stop her ourselves.'

Nicko sighed, but didn't argue. 'All right, then, maybe *we* can persuade Annie not to do it at school. Only the other Reception kids have heard her so far, and nobody takes any notice of them anyway.'

'We'll have to try.' The thought of everyone at school, including psychos like Bonehead Griffiths, finding out about Sarah Slade made Jack break out into a cold sweat. He would have no chance of keeping Annie out of trouble for the next two and a half weeks if she and Sarah went public. None at all.

'I'd better go,' Nicko said. 'We'll talk to her tomorrow, all right?'

Jack nodded.

'And I'm going to have a nose around Annie's bedroom tonight, when she's out of the way. See what I can find . . .'

The trouble was, he wasn't quite sure what he was looking for. When Jack inched his way carefully into Annie's bedroom later that evening, he stopped uncertainly just inside the door, wondering what he was doing there. His mother was washing Annie's hair in the bathroom next door, and he could hear them discussing what would happen if a person never washed her hair at all. Their mother was maintaining strongly that the said person's hair would all drop out eventually, while Annie's theory was that the hair would become self-cleaning. At any rate, they were debating the issue so loudly, they didn't know that Jack was in Annie's bedroom next door.

Jack picked his way uneasily through the silver buildings which were crammed into the floor space. He felt strangely spooked, as if he was being watched. Telling himself not to be so stupid, he glanced round the bedroom, searching desperately for clues. Annie might have written something down or drawn a picture which might tell him more about exactly what was going on inside her head.

With a muffled exclamation, Jack suddenly froze in mid-air, one foot mere millimetres off the ground. He'd been about to put his left trainer down on the plasticine model of Sarah Slade, which was lying on the rug in front of him. That would have given him away for sure. Carefully he placed his feet either side of it, and squatted down. Next to the model of Sarah was the tiny plasticine saxophone. Jack stared at it grimly. Close by the saxophone was the model of his mum's Filofax, with Nicko's glasses lying on top of it. It was then that he noticed the red plasticine book in one of Sarah's hands, and the white-and-black plasticine football in the other.

'Hmm,' Nicko said thoughtfully when Jack told him what he'd seen. They were on the way to school the following morning. Annie was trailing a little way behind them, chatting to Sarah, so it was safe to talk. 'A book and a football. It's hardly earth-shattering stuff, is it?'

'Yes, but why are they there?' Jack glanced behind them to make sure Annie couldn't hear what they were saying. She was discussing the EU with Sarah, and making two old-age pensioners who were walking along behind her very nervous indeed. 'You know what it means when Sarah's got a new model.' He lowered his voice. 'It means Annie's at it again.'

'Oh, come on,' said Nicko. 'You haven't had a book or a football nicked, have you?'

'No.'

'Well, then.'

'So why is she making the models?'

'To wind you up?' Nicko suggested gently. 'You said that's why she was doing it.'

Jack thought about it. Nicko was right. Annie

couldn't have stolen those things. Where would she have got them from? She wasn't allowed out on her own, and they didn't belong to anyone in their house. She might have taken them from a friend, but she didn't have any friends.

'Did you speak to her about Sarah yet?' Nicko asked him. 'About not talking to her at school?'

Jack shook his head. 'I thought we could do that together.'

Nicko glanced back over his shoulder. 'Better do it now,' he advised. 'Those two old ladies behind us look absolutely terrified.'

Jack grinned. 'Come here, Annie,' he called over his shoulder.

Annie gave the two pensioners a dazzling smile, which made them hurry off, looking alarmed. Then she ran and caught up with her brother and Nicko. Immediately the smile vanished from her face.

'You were in my room last night, Jack.'

Jack looked uncomfortable. 'No, I wasn't.'

'Yes, you were. You were in my room last night when Mummy was washing my hair. Sarah just told me so.'

Jack couldn't even deny it, because he couldn't speak. His tongue seemed to have swollen, and stuck to the roof of his mouth. There was no way Annie could have known that he'd been in her bedroom. He hadn't touched anything, he hadn't disturbed anything, he hadn't taken anything away . . .

'I don't want you to go in there again,' Annie said sternly. 'So keep out.'

She must have set some sort of trap for him, Jack realized suddenly. Of course. A hair across the doorknob, or a tiny bit of paper balanced somewhere. Or maybe he'd knocked one of the silver buildings ever so slightly out of place when he'd stepped over them. There had to be a simple explanation, and there was. And to think, for one second – no, he hadn't *really* begun to believe in Sarah Slade . . .

'Never mind that,' he said quickly. 'We want to talk to you.'

Annie yawned delicately. 'About what?'

'It's just a suggestion,' Nicko said. 'But we think you might find it easier if you don't talk to Sarah when we're at school.'

Annie raised one eyebrow at them, and Jack felt extremely irritated. He'd never been able to do that, however much he practised.

'Why?'

'Because the other kids will think—' Jack caught Nicko's eye, and faltered. He'd been about to say that the other kids would think she was a nutter, but that was probably a bit too blunt. 'Because the other kids will think you're a bit – er – strange,' he offered weakly.

103

'Oh,' Annie said thoughtfully.

'After all, the other kids can't see Sarah, so they won't understand,' Nicko pointed out reasonably. 'Do you see what we mean?'

'Oh, yes.' Annie nodded. 'Yes I do.'

They were getting closer to the school now. It was almost time for the bell to ring, and there was a large crowd of children, juniors and infants, hovering around the gates.

'So you'll stop talking to Sarah at school then,' Jack asked eagerly.

Annie gave him a cool smile.

'No, I can't do that,' she said. Then she held out her hand as if she was grabbing someone else's, and yelled, 'Come on, Sarah, I'll race you to the other end of the playground! I bet I win!'

She ran off, her hair flying, and there was a stunned silence behind her. The whole crowd of children at the gate had fallen quiet, and were standing around with their mouths open like a choir frozen in mid-note. Jack had time for one short, agonized glance at Nicko before the storm broke around them.

'Did you see that? She was talking, and there wasn't anybody there!'

Some of the children, especially the younger ones, still looked bewildered, but most of the others were laughing now, and shooting sly glances at Jack. He felt himself colour a bright, scarlet red, slowly and remorselessly, from his chin up to the roots of his hair.

'Your sister's a loony!' someone shouted. Jack tried to see who it was, but there was a dark mist in front of his eyes. Then he felt Nicko's fingers close around his wrist, and drag him away.

'She did that on purpose!' Jack pulled away from Nicko when they reached the safety of the back of the school, and ran his hands frenziedly through his hair. 'She did that on purpose, in front of all those kids!'

Nicko looked at him helplessly.

'This is going to be all round the school in the next ten minutes,' Jack said through his teeth. 'Why did she do it?'

'Don't ask me.' Nicko's face was white. They both stared hopelessly across the playground, where Annie was holding hands with no-one at all and whirling round and round in circles, ignoring the crowd of sniggering kids standing round her.

'Stop it, Sarah!' she was giggling, 'You're making me dizzy!'

Unable to tear his eyes away, his heart heavy with foreboding, Jack watched her twirling round. Why was she doing this to him? He just didn't deserve it. But as he watched his tiny sister happily turning circle after circle in the middle of all those sneering kids, he felt something he didn't feel very often for Annie. Pity.

But when the bell rang for the beginning of morning school, Jack began to feel sorrier for himself than for Annie. Walking down the long corridor, past all the cloakrooms, to their classroom, was like running a gauntlet. Kids popped their heads round doors and out of the cloakrooms as he and Nicko went by, giggling and sneering, and occasionally calling out rude remarks about Annie. Jack didn't answer any of them. He kept going, his eyes fixed on their classroom at the end of the corridor. He was glad that Nicko was right beside him, their shoulders touching slightly in a gesture of solidarity.

'Hey, Robinson. Word is, your sister's a complete nutter.'

Bonehead Griffiths stepped out of the Year Six cloakroom almost *gracefully*, Jack thought in a detached way. Certainly he must have been lurking there on the look-out for them, because he'd timed his move to block their path to perfection.

'Say that again, Bonehead,' Jack suggested almost casually. He felt Nicko tense beside him.

'Your sister's a nutter,' Bonehead repeated loudly. His mates, who were draped around the cloakroom walls, sniggered obligingly. Silently children began to drift towards them from other parts of the corridor.

'She is not.' The dark mist was swirling in front of Jack's eyes again, but through it he could see Bonehead quite clearly, as if he was looking through one of those pinhole cameras they'd made in class a few months ago. It was funny, he thought calmly, but he'd never noticed before just how essentially stupid Bonehead looked. It was the combination of that round, fleshy face, the dull but beady eyes that missed nothing and the slack, narrow-lipped mouth. His nickname had been coined by a student teacher their class had had a year or two ago. The student, frustrated by Basil's stubborn refusal to learn, had, rather unprofessionally, called him a bonehead. Basil had been rather proud of the name, and had adopted it full-time. It suited him, Jack thought, smiling to himself.

'What're you grinning at, Robinson?' Bonehead's face darkened. He reached forward and gave Jack a tiny, challenging push with his forefinger. 'Your sister's a nutter. She's talking to people who aren't there.'

'Shut up, Bonehead.' Jack felt a flame of anger catch light inside him.

'She's a nutter,' Bonehead said with a snigger. One of the few things he was expert at was needling people, and he could tell that Jack was on the edge. It was therefore Bonehead's duty to push him right over. 'She ought to be locked up.'

'Shut your mouth, Bonehead,' Jack said quietly. 'Or I'll shut it for you.'

He heard Nicko's sharp intake of breath, and behind them the crowd of kids rustled with anticipation. No-one had had a fist fight with Bonehead for almost two years. The last person who'd had that honour, Richard Kennedy, had passed into school legend, because afterwards he'd needed fourteen stitches and a false tooth. Since then, Bonehead had reigned as undisputed heavyweight champion of the school.

'Oh, yeah?' A huge grin split Bonehead's face. He shaded his eyes with his hand, and looked in an exaggerated manner up and down the corridor. 'You and whose army, Robinson?'

The children standing around laughed nervously. Bonehead's chest swelled with pride. He might be dumb at Maths and useless at English, but this was something he was good at.

'Come on then, Robinson.' He took a step towards Jack, encouraging the other boy forward with small movements of his hands. 'Come on then. Shut my mouth for me.'

The mist in front of Jack's eyes got darker. He heard Nicko hiss, 'Leave it, Jack,' but he couldn't leave it. With all the misery and frustration of the last few days propelling him forward, he launched himself full-tilt at Bonehead.

The moment of contact with Bonehead was pure release. As he shoved at the other boy and Bonehead staggered, Jack felt a peace flood through him that was as cool and clear as a mountain stream. The feeling lasted only for seconds. Then Bonehead rallied, and flung one arm around Jack, trying to steady him, so that he could punch him with the other. The watching crowd was screaming encouragement now, although Jack couldn't make out what they were saying. He tried to wriggle out of the bear-hug he was trapped in, but he couldn't. The sheer strength of Bonehead's grip was terrifying him. He would never have believed that a boy of his own age could be so strong. Like a small animal mesmerized by a swaying snake, Jack froze in Bonehead's grasp, watching the large, clenched fist hovering above his head, choosing a contact point. He closed his eyes.

'What's going on here?'

By the time Mr Daniels had finished speaking, everyone had melted away like ice in a heat wave, even Bonehead's gang. Within twenty seconds, the only people left in the corridor were Jack, Bonehead, Nicko and the headmaster.

'Go into class, please, Nicholas,' said Mr

Daniels. Nicko caught Jack's eye briefly, and went.

'Follow me, please.' Mr Daniels marched the two boys into the nearby library. It was empty, and he clicked the door shut behind them. 'What was all that about, please? Jack? Basil?'

'Nothing, sir,' they said together. Bonehead flicked a suspicious look sideways at Jack, but Jack kept quiet. He had what Daniels would probably consider a pretty good reason for losing his temper, but he didn't want to start a fuss about Annie. As far as Jack could tell, the teachers hadn't caught on to Annie's relationship with Sarah yet. But when they did, trouble would inevitably follow. And if they then got onto his mum, maybe said that Annie shouldn't go to see her father until her other problems were sorted out first . . . Jack swallowed down the fear that leapt up inside him.

'It was nothing, sir,' he muttered again. Mr Daniels gave him a puzzled look, and then talked for five minutes about how fighting was considered a serious offence in school. They were both given three lunchtime detentions. Then Bonehead was sent back to class.

'Not you, Jack,' Mr Daniels said, as he made to leave too. 'I want to talk to you.'

Bonehead went out of the library, giving Jack

another suspicious look, and banging the door shut behind him.

'Straight back to class, please, Basil,' Mr Daniels called. He and Jack waited a moment or two in silence, a silence that stretched Jack's nerves to screeching-point. He was just wondering whether he was expected to say something – anything – to break the agonizing quiet, when Mr Daniels padded silently over to the door, and pulled it open. Bonehead fell into the room.

'Just doing my shoelace up, sir,' he said in an injured tone.

'Goodbye, Basil.' Mr Daniels watched Bonehead shamble off up the corridor, looking aggrieved. Then he turned to Jack.

'I hate clichés, Jack. You know what clichés are, don't you?' Jack nodded. 'But I'm going to use one anyway. This isn't like you.'

Jack's eyes dropped. 'Sorry, sir.'

'It isn't an apology I'm looking for. I just want to know why.'

Jack studied the carpet while the clock above them ticked away in the silence. Mr Daniels sighed audibly.

'Your mother's told me about your trip,' he said. 'You must be very excited about seeing your father again after all this time.'

Fear closed up Jack's throat.

'Yes,' he managed to say. Oh, God, was the headmaster going to tell his mum he'd been fighting? She'd go mad. She might even blame his dad for getting in touch. She might make out that his dad's phone call after all this time had unsettled him. Made him do stupid things. Then the trip would definitely be off.

'You must be nervous, too, you and your sister.' Mr Daniels waited to see if Jack would say anything, and when he didn't, went on delicately. 'If you want to talk to anyone, Jack, about anything at all, there's always someone here.'

'Thanks, sir.' Jack started edging towards the door. Daniels was making it sound like *he* was the one who had the problem, he thought indignantly, when none of this was any of his fault. It was all down to Annie. But he was going to have to be careful in future. It looked like he'd got away with it this time. But he couldn't allow himself to get into any more fights. His mother would go mad, and she might even cancel their trip if she thought *he* was getting unsettled at the thought of seeing his father again. That would be ironic.

It was two and a half weeks until they left. How much can happen in two and a half weeks? Jack asked himself silently as he went back to class. Dismally he answered his own question – a lot. Somehow he had to try to stop the other kids from teasing Annie, before the teachers found out about Sarah, and started interfering. How?

The word throbbed inside Jack's head as he walked slowly back to class.

How? How? How?

CHAPTER SIX

It only took Jack the rest of the day to realize that, although everything that was happening was Annie's fault, she wasn't getting the worst of it. He was.

The Reception class was right at the far end of the school. The infants had different playtimes, going out fifteen minutes before the juniors and going back inside on the same bell which sent the juniors out. Although they shared the same lunch hour, during lunch time the infants were confined to one section of the playground, and the juniors to another. The dividing line between the two, invisible but observed solemnly by everyone just the same, was

114

patrolled by one of a rare species, a fearsome dinner lady. There were always plenty of people hovering around in the infants too; parents helping with reading, part-time assistants, pupils from the local comprehensive doing work experience. Lots of people around to step in when any kind of teasing started up. Not so in the juniors. Annie, Jack thought bitterly, was cocooned from the worst of the Sarah Slade backlash. He wasn't.

It started up again when he went back to class after the session with Daniels. His class teacher, Mrs Reeves, had been disappointed in him. She hadn't said anything to him except that. 'I'm disappointed in you, Jack,' she'd said quietly when she'd given him his Maths book. No-one else had heard, but Jack's face had flamed. He liked Mrs Reeves. He'd had a crush on her years ago, when he was seven.

Most of the other children in the class had giggled and sniggered and made comments, of course. Some, who were more sensitive, tried to question Jack quite seriously, but Jack thought that this was worse than the sniggering, in a way. He appreciated their attempts to understand, but he didn't want to talk about it.

Then there was Bonehead. The note, crumpled and dirty, had arrived on Jack's desk halfway through Maths. *Your sister is a nutter*, it read.

Actually, to be accurate, it said *Your sister is a nuter*. Jack got up, pretending he was hunting for an eraser, and dropped the note on Bonehead's desk when Mrs Reeves wasn't looking.

'There are two Ts in nutter, Bonehead,' he said quietly.

'Are there?' Bonehead said, then his face turned purple at being caught out. 'What're you telling me for?' he blustered.

Jack went back to his desk, and saw that Nicko was watching him anxiously from the other side of the room. They always sat together but Mrs Reeves had split them up today because of Jack's fight with Bonehead. As he bent his head over the maths he couldn't concentrate on, Jack thought that being separated from Nicko was the worst punishment of all, worse than being in trouble with Mr Daniels and with Mrs Reeves, worse than three detentions and worse than putting up with Bonehead.

'What happened?' was all Nicko said when they finally met up at playtime, but his eyes were full of concern.

'I got three detentions, and so did Bonehead.' Jack looked warily over his shoulder to check that they were alone. They'd gone round the back of the canteen behind the kitchens, which wasn't a popular place because the huge steel bins there stank of mouldy food.

'You should have told Daniels what Bonehead said.'

'No. I don't want any of the teachers to know.' Jack kicked moodily at the base of one of the bins. 'Nicko, you've got to help me. We've got to make sure Annie doesn't talk to Sarah at school, and if she does, we've got to make sure the other kids don't get a chance to pick on her. That just makes her worse.'

Nicko looked blank. 'How do we do that?'

Jack thought hard. 'We've got to minimize the amount of time she's with the other kids without any teachers around,' he said slowly. 'That means we've got to get to school late in the mornings, and get her out as fast as we can at night.'

Nicko looked doubtful. 'It might work . . . But for how long? The teachers are bound to wise up sooner or later. And then—'

'And then they'll have to interfere. That's what teachers do.' Jack paced nervously up and down. 'Daniels might tell my mum that maybe it's best if Annie doesn't go to America. They might think she needs help or something to get rid of Sarah.'

Nicko cleared his throat.

'Maybe she does,' he said tentatively.

'No.' Jack was shaking his head, even though

117

a seed of doubt was busy sowing itself inside his mind. No. There were only three possible explanations for the presence of Sarah Slade in their lives. One, Sarah was real. Two, Annie, with her incredible imagination and her mind-blowing IQ, genuinely *thought* she was real. Or three, Annie was doing it to wind them all up. One was obviously out; two was possible, but Jack didn't want to believe it. He'd go for three, any day. Number three was a simpler situation, one he could deal with on his own without any interference from grown-ups. But a small voice kept nagging away at the back of his mind, saying, 'What if it's more serious than that?'

The rest of the day improved in that it went from very bad to simply bad. During the course of lessons, Jack received a further six notes, all penned in Bonehead's inimitable style, and ranging from *Your sister is a luny* to *Your sister's a nutter, and so are your mum and dad and so are YOU!* The word 'nutter' was now spelt correctly, although 'loony' wasn't. The final lesson of the day for Year Six was singing practice with Mr Ryder, the music teacher. Bonehead and his gang were standing behind Jack in the hall, and they made up new versions of every song they sang, with variations on the same basic theme of Jack's sister being a nutter.

So Jack had braced himself for confrontation

in the playground after school, but although a fair-sized gang of children did hang around for a while, hoping for further Sarah Slade revelations from his sister, the Reception class was late out again. They'd had Games last lesson, and most of them were still struggling into their clothes long after the home bell had gone. By the time Miss Turner, pale with the effort of tying thirty-one pairs of shoelaces, let her class out into the playground, most of the other children had got bored and left, even Bonehead and his mates.

Jack and Nicko were waiting right beside the Reception class door. As soon as Annie came out, they scooped her up, and hustled her out of the playground. There were a few insults thrown at them from a couple of die-hard busybodies who were still hanging around the school gates, but they ignored them, and bore Annie off down the street. Once they'd turned the corner and the Robinsons' house was in sight, Jack and Nicko both let out sighs of relief and slowed down.

'Can I have my feet back now, please?' Annie asked grumpily. 'They haven't touched the ground since I came out of the classroom.'

'Sorry.' Jack let go of her arm. 'You were late, and we just wanted to get you home, so Mum didn't worry.'

Annie didn't reply. She knew her brother

was lying, but it wasn't worth saying so. Jack looked tired and pale, and he had dark circles under his eyes. Annie looked just as bad, and anyone seeing her in this state would probably have been overcome by a desire to pick her up and cuddle her. Jack knew that their mum would do that when they got home, but it would never occur to him even to reach out for her hand. Jack never held Annie's hand unless it was simply an automatic gesture to make sure she kept up with him.

Annie felt just like Jeffrey, the black-and-white cat who lived next door to them. Jeffrey often ignored Annie, who adored him, and instead made a determined beeline for Mrs Robinson, who had an allergy to fur and didn't want him anywhere near her. Annie always felt like that when she was with Jack, trying to attract the attention of someone who wasn't interested in her. Annie sighed, almost silently.

'You had a fight with that Basil Griffiths, didn't you?'

'Bonehead, you mean.' Jack looked cautious. There was no way he wanted their mother to get wind of this. 'And it wasn't a fight. Just an argument.'

Annie raised an eyebrow. 'Sarah said it was a fight,' she remarked, and walked off towards the house.

'Sarah?' Nicko repeated nervously.

'One of the other kids must have told her. Obviously.' Jack started after Annie. 'I've got to go, Nicko. I've got to make sure she doesn't say anything to my mum.'

'See you tomorrow morning then.'

'Yes, but—' Jack stopped, thinking ahead swiftly. 'Make it later than usual. Then we can get Annie straight into class.'

The look on Nicko's face showed that he understood. Jack ran up the path after his sister, prepared for some serious damage limitation. If Annie mentioned the fight to their mother, he'd have to talk his way out of it somehow.

'Annie!' He caught her at the door, as she was about to ring the bell.

'What?'

'Don't say anything to Mum about Bonehead, all right?' Jack looked sternly at her. 'If you keep quiet, I won't tell her you've been talking to Sarah at school.'

They stared challengingly at each other for a few seconds. Then Annie shrugged.

'All right.'

Jack felt a spasm of relief. So far so good. He found his doorkey, and they went in.

Their mother was in the kitchen, making sandwiches. 'Hello, you two. Had a good day?'

'Yes,' Jack said quickly, then held his breath,

121

as his mother looked at Annie. Annie didn't answer.

'Annie?' Their mother frowned at her. 'Did you have a good day, sweetheart?'

Jack's heart began to bang. He glanced sideways at his sister.

'Oh, yes, thank you,' Annie said, looking up with wide, innocent eyes. 'I didn't hear what you said.'

Jack glared at his sister as she went over to sit at the table. She'd done that on purpose, to make him sweat.

'Come and sit down.' Their mother carried some plates over to the table. 'I've made you something to eat.'

Jack sat down, as far away from Annie as he could get. It was then that he noticed the airline tickets lying on the dresser.

'Dad sorted out the tickets!' Jack's face lit up. He leaned over and picked the tickets up, leafing through them just to make sure they were real. His father had got that done really quickly, he thought happily, it had only taken him about a week. Obviously his dad was as keen to see Jack, as Jack was to see him.

Jack felt a joyful warmth spread right through him. Now that the tickets were actually in his hand, he could allow himself to admit that he hadn't been 100 per cent sure that his father would get around to arranging things. He remembered quite clearly, although he was experienced at pushing the bad memories away, that his dad had never been very efficient at organizing things. Or good with money.

'Yes. I picked them up from the travel agents this morning.' His mother had her back to Jack, slicing cheese, and he noticed nothing odd in her voice. 'Annie, do you want another sandwich?'

'No, thank you.' Annie slid out from behind the table, and went upstairs. Jack sat back in his chair and ate his sandwich, and relaxed. Now that the tickets were here, there were only two more weeks at school to get through. Only two weeks, and then they'd be gone. Then they would be in America for seventeen days, and a lot could happen in seventeen days. Annie might get fed up with Sarah, for instance, and start a new game. And then, by the time they got back, the other kids would probably have forgotten all about her imaginary friend.

Jack relaxed still further. The only problem he now faced was keeping Annie out of trouble until they left. And if he and Nicko could co-ordinate their movements as well as they'd done that evening to get Annie out of school as fast as they could, it should be all right.

The plan for next morning worked well, too.

'You're going to be late if you don't leave now,' his mother warned Jack as she stood in front of the hall mirror, putting her make-up on before she left for work. 'You're both ready, aren't you?'

'Yes, but Nicko's not here yet,' Jack said innocently.

'He might be ill.' His mother clicked her lipstick case shut, and glanced at her watch. 'Don't wait for him. Get Annie, and go.'

'We're going to be late,' Annie said, hurtling down the stairs towards them. Jack saw that she had the plasticine model of Sarah Slade in her hand, and that the book and the football Sarah had been holding had been replaced by a tiny doll and what looked like a baseball cap. A vague unease shivered through him. He pushed it aside.

'Here's Nicko now.' Their mother scooped up her car keys, as a shadow fell across the glass. 'Go on, you'll have to run.'

'You cut it a bit fine today,' Jack muttered to Nicko as he and Annie went outside. 'My mum was just about to send us on our own.'

'Sorry, I thought you wanted me to be late!' Nicko grinned. 'We'll have to run for it.'

They arrived at school just as the bell was ringing and the children were going inside. Nicko and Jack managed to escort Annie down to the Reception class without incident, both of them breathing a sigh of relief as they reached the cloakroom, where Miss Turner was standing guard, untangling mittens on strings.

'Bye,' Annie said, detaching her elbows from their grip. 'I feel like a film star with all my bodyguards.' Then she disappeared into the heaving mass in the cloakroom.

Nicko looked uneasily at Jack. 'She knows what we're up to then.'

'Looks like it.' Jack shrugged. He didn't really care one way or another. His plan was working, and he'd got the incredible, euphoric feeling that things were actually getting better. Nothing happened to shake this feeling either when he and Nicko got to class. Because they were so late, Mrs Reeves came in right behind them, carrying the register, so there was no time for anyone, not even Bonehead, to make any annoying remarks. Jack was allowed to sit next to Nicko again, and everything was back to normal.

It was only when Assembly came round after Mrs Reeves had taken the register, that Jack felt a second twinge of unease. When his class filed into the hall, the Reception class were already in there, sitting right at the front in straggly rows. Jack searched for Annie straightaway, and spotted her sitting at the end of the front line. She looked quite composed, sitting with her legs crossed neatly in the way that teachers approved of ('On your *bottom*, please, Justin,' Miss Turner was saying despairingly to one child who kept rearing up onto his knees).

Jack couldn't help wondering if Annie had deliberately wangled a place at the end of a row so that there was room for Sarah to sit down next to her. Apart from that, he wasn't sure why he felt uneasy. Annie wasn't likely to do anything strange in the middle of Assembly. She wouldn't dare.

At first, Assembly was all right. Mr Daniels read them a story, and then they sang a couple of songs. After the singing was over, Mr Daniels read out the notices. There were reports about a football match, swimming certificates to be given out and a message from the caretaker, deploring the amount of toilet paper that was being shoved down the lavatories and blocking the drains. Then Mr Daniels paused. His face gradually assumed an even more serious look than the blocked drains had warranted, and everyone in the hall sat up straight. They all knew that look. Something very important was about to be said.

'Before you all go back to class, I want to talk to you about something very serious.' Mr Daniels paused again, milking the silence to the last drop. 'I've left it until last because it is so very serious, and I want you all to go away and think about it when Assembly is over.' The silence was so intense, it felt as if no-one was even breathing. 'I'm afraid to say that we have a thief here in our school.'

Jack was listening intently along with everyone else. Then, suddenly, a slow, freezing wave of realization began to sweep remorselessly over him.

'It's been a long time since we've had stealing on this scale at Mansfield.' Mr Daniels' gaze raked the rows of silent children, almost as if he was expecting the culprit to jump up and admit the crime there and then. 'But so many items have suddenly disappeared over the last couple of days, it seems clear that just one person is the thief. And several more things have disappeared this morning.'

Jack knew he was shaking from head to foot, but he couldn't control it. Not wanting to draw any attention to himself, he nevertheless couldn't stop himself from looking round at Nicko, who was sitting beside him. He could tell from Nicko's face that the other boy hadn't yet realized the significance of what Daniels was saying. He caught Nicko's eye, and stared at him, knowing his face was burning with the dreadful knowledge that was throbbing in his brain. Then he saw the colour drain quickly from

Nicko's face, as if someone had pulled out a plug inside his head, and he could see his own terrible thoughts mirrored in his friend's eyes.

Mr Daniels was now giving a short lecture on why stealing had no place at Mansfield Primary, and the very serious consequences for anyone who was caught in the act.

'Will everyone please think about what I've said, especially the thief. He or she knows who they are.' His gaze swept over the assembled children for the last time. 'Will Miss Turner's class please stand?'

Jack's eyes locked onto his sister as she stood up with the rest of the Reception class. As Annie led them out of the hall, she turned to look at him, just once, but Jack thought he saw defiance in her face. Or maybe he just imagined it.

'Jack.' Nicko was fidgeting wildly beside him. 'You don't think—'

'Not here. Wait until we get out.'

Back in class, both boys asked Mrs Reeves if they could collect something from their coat pockets. Mrs Reeves agreed easily, thinking they were concerned about the unknown thief. Two minutes later the boys met up in the cloakroom, both of them pale and wide-eyed.

'It's Annie, isn't it?' Nicko said, his voice shaking. 'You think Annie's the thief.'

'Everything fits.' Jack could hear his own

voice shaking too. 'Some of the kids have been upsetting her, so she's stolen their things. Just like before.'

'We don't know that for sure. Daniels didn't say who'd had their stuff nicked.'

'Yes, but she made those plasticine models as well, didn't she? I told you I'd seen them. They were models of kids' things. I saw two when I went into her bedroom the other day, and two this morning, but there must be more. I haven't been checking.'

'But Daniels didn't say what had been taken, either.'

'No. And we can't risk asking around. So we won't know until we get a chance to talk to Annie.' Jack could hear the tension in his own voice. If Annie was the thief, if she was caught in the act, he could wave goodbye to their American trip. 'We'll talk to her tonight, after school.'

Nicko looked at Jack with wide tragic eyes.

'I hope it isn't her.'

'So do I.' But Jack knew it was. It had to be. He turned away and put his hand into his coat pocket. There was a ping-pong ball in there that he'd been carrying around for the last month, although he wasn't quite sure why. 'Have you got something you can take back to class, so Reeves doesn't get suspicious?'

Nicko found his jacket, fumbled in the pocket

and produced a half-eaten packet of Polo mints.

'I still can't believe it. I mean, *Annie . . .*' His voice tailed away.

Jack didn't want to believe it either. But he did, because it all fitted in so beautifully. It was all part of Annie's game. People who annoyed and upset her had to be punished.

Although interest in Sarah Slade was still at its height, Jack found it easier to cope with all the sarcastic comments because now he had something much more important on his mind. He even found it easy enough to ignore Bonehead's muttered insults as he went over to the pencil sharpener near Jack's desk for the fortieth time. The day dragged on, through his lunch time detention, silent reading and art, until the home bell rang.

Disaster hit without warning at three twelve that afternoon, three minutes before the home bell.

'I need two people to stay behind for ten minutes or so to wash up the paint pots,' Mrs Reeves said, looking round the classroom for volunteers. There weren't any. 'Jack and Nicholas, I think it's your turn.'

The two boys glanced at each other in horror.

'We've got to go to football practice, Miss,' Jack blurted out, off the top of his head.

Mrs Reeves raised her eyebrows.

'What day is it today, Jack?'

'Friday, miss,' Jack muttered, knowing exactly what she was going to say.

'Football practice, to my knowledge, has always been on Mondays,' Mrs Reeves remarked mildly. 'Get started now, and you'll be finished in a few minutes. The rest of you may go.'

While the rest of the children went out, Jack and Nicko washed quickly and efficiently at the classroom sink in strained silence. Jack had taken his watch off and left it on a nearby cupboard, but he kept glancing at it every few seconds. They were over ten minutes late. Annie was bound to be out in the playground by now. He didn't want to think about what could be happening out there.

Annie was not only out, she was surrounded by a crowd of children. There were so many of them around that some of the kids in the outer circles couldn't see her, and they were hopping up and down impatiently on the outskirts of the crowd. The most frightening thing was that none of the children were making a sound. Jack and Nicko stopped in dismay as they took in what was happening, then, by mutual consent, they broke into a run. Jack's insides turned over unpleasantly as he saw that the inner circle, the people that were closest to Annie, was composed of Bonehead and his mates. His second glance told him that Bonehead was incandescent with rage, his face mottled with purple.

'Hello, Jack,' Annie said cheerfully, as he shouldered his way through the crowd toward her. She looked very small and slight in the middle of Bonehead and his hulking gang. 'Can we go home now?'

'Yes.' Jack grabbed her wrist, not looking at Bonehead, wondering what Annie had said to him to make him turn the colour of a pickled beetroot. They had a problem now. To break out of the circle, they would have to push past the enraged Bonehead and his cronies. Jack didn't move. Instead he looked down at his feet, and prayed silently for a teacher to appear. They were like buses, never around when you needed one, and then two or three always appeared together. Sure enough, as Bonehead moved towards him and Annie, fists clenched and mute with anger, Mr Daniels strolled round the corner of the school, chatting to Mr Ryder.

The crowd scattered. Bonehead was last to move.

'Monday, Robinson,' he said in a voice suffused with rage. 'Monday.' Then he too was gone.

'What have you been saying to Bonehead?' Jack hissed as he dragged Annie across the playground with Nicko close behind them.

'Jack, you're hurting me.' Annie pulled away from him. 'I didn't say anything. He was asking me about Sarah, so I told him.'

'What did you tell him?'

'Oh, all about the twenty-fifth century.' Annie yawned, obviously uninterested. 'Then Sarah started talking to me, and he asked me what she was saying.'

'And?'

'I told him that Sarah said he was a perfect example of matter over mind.' Annie giggled. 'He didn't understand that, so I explained it to him. He wasn't very pleased.'

'I'll bet,' Nicko muttered. 'You should keep away from Bonehead, Annie. He's dangerous.'

Annie shrugged. 'Sarah wouldn't let him hurt me,' she said confidently.

'Never mind that now.' Jack pushed the awful prospect of Bonehead's revenge after the weekend to the back of his mind. First things first. 'Nicko and I want to talk to you.'

Annie let out an exaggerated sigh. 'Again?'

'Yes, again. And you know what this is about.'

Annie's eyes shuttered. She turned away. 'No, I don't.'

'Yes, you do.' Jack yanked her round to face him, none too gently. Annie squeaked in protest.

'Go easy, Jack,' Nicko said nervously.

'You're the thief.' Jack didn't trust himself to say any more.

Annie's eyes widened. 'I am NOT.'

'All right. Then it's Sarah.'

Annie's indignant gaze wavered. 'You don't believe in Sarah,' she said accusingly.

'Is it Sarah?' Jack fixed his eyes on her. If Annie said it was Sarah, for him that was just as good as admitting that she'd done it herself.

Annie stared him right between the eyes.

'Yes.'

Jack felt a cold hand grasp his heart.

'Because those kids were teasing you?'

'Yes,' Annie said defiantly. Then she turned and walked off.

'Oh, God,' Jack heard Nicko say quietly. He didn't say anything, because, quite suddenly out of nowhere, an idea had come to him. It was a monstrous idea and it went against all the laws of nature, but it was still a good idea. It might just work.

It had to work.

CHAPTER SEVEN

'Bonehead?'

Jack's voice was a squeak of fear. Quickly he tried again, pitching his voice a little deeper.

'Bonehead?'

Bonehead was sitting alone on the flat canteen roof, having used the tall steel dustbins as stepping stones. Jack knew that he would be there, which was why he'd come to school early today. Bonehead was always on the canteen roof every Monday morning from 7.15 onwards. Some of the kids said that Bonehead's mum got so fed up with him over the weekend, she threw him out of the house every Monday morning at seven o'clock. Jack didn't know if that was true or not.

'Hello, Robinson.' Bonehead peered down at Jack from above, and a malevolent grin slowly lit up his face. 'You've saved me the bother of coming to look for you.' He stood up, strolled across the roof and let himself down with a noisy clang onto the nearest dustbin lid. Jack's knees buckled underneath him. He was taking a gamble, and it was a gamble he had to win.

He wished Nicko was with him, for moral support. But he'd asked Nicko to collect Annie, and come along later. Of course, Nicko had wanted to know why Jack wanted to get to school so early on Monday morning, so Jack had made up a story about wanting to check out some books about America in the school library. There were two reasons why Jack hadn't wanted to tell Nicko the truth. One, because he wasn't sure he could pull it off, and two, because he knew that Nicko would be shocked and try to talk him out of it. But although Jack knew that what he was about to do was bizarre, unnatural and probably illegal, he didn't want to be talked out of it either. It was his only chance.

Bonehead leapt off the top of the dustbin, setting the lid rattling menacingly. Then he walked slowly over to Jack, aggression rampant in every line of his body.

'All right, Robinson,' he growled. 'Let's finish what your sister started on Friday.'

Jack held his ground, even though every primitive instinct in his body was urging him to turn round and run like fury.

'I want to talk to you,' he said.

Bonehead kept on coming.

'No violence, Bonehead.' Jack tried desperately to assume a bored expression. 'I said I wanted to talk to you. This is business.'

Bonehead stopped, looking suspicious. Jack half-expected him to say, 'Violence *is* my business,' as if he was in a Hollywood movie, but Bonehead didn't. He seemed to be having some difficulty dealing with the concept of conversation instead of fisticuffs.

'What business?' he asked at last.

'I've got a proposition to put to you,' Jack said quickly. Step one was accomplished. He'd got Bonehead listening. Now he had to persuade him to agree, or within two minutes he, Jack Robinson, would become intimately acquainted with the concrete surface of the school playground.

'Do what?'

'I want to make you an offer . . .' An offer I'm praying you won't refuse, or I'm history. 'I want you to do something for me.'

Bonehead looked blank for a second. Then an expression of supremely righteous indignation spread slowly across his face.

'You what?' His fists clenched. 'I'm gonna take you out right now, Robinson. You've got a nerve. What makes you think I'd do anything for you, you dirty little—'

'I'll pay you.'

Bonehead blinked several times. 'Say that again.'

'I'll pay you,' Jack repeated more confidently. He had Bonehead on a hook now, and he was about to reel him in. He knew it.

Bonehead was struggling now with two different temptations: violence as opposed to financial gain. His heart thundering, Jack watched Bonehead wavering between the two, his titanic struggle mirrored in his eyes. At last the other boy spoke.

'I'll do it.'

'I haven't told you what it is yet.' Jack tried to stop himself from sagging too obviously with relief.

'Doesn't matter.' Bonehead grinned, which was rather like a Rottweiler that was about to bite your hand off suddenly beginning to wag its tail. 'Tell me what it is, and I'll do it.'

Jack felt cautiously triumphant. He thought he was home and dry, but there was still a faint chance that Bonehead might turn nasty. When it came to intimidation, Bonehead's unpredictable moods were one of his greatest assets.

'All right. You know my sister's getting teased by some of the other kids?'

'Yeah.' Bonehead immediately looked suspicious again, as well he might, seeing that he was one of the principal tormentors.

'Well, I want you to stop them.'

Bonehead looked bewildered.

'I want you to stop them,' Jack said again. 'You and your mates.'

'What, give them all a going-over, you mean?' Bonehead asked, his eyes wide.

'No,' Jack said quickly. 'No violence or you don't get paid.' This was bizarre, he thought weakly, but he pressed on. 'Just a bit of quiet intimidation.'

Bonehead looked blank.

'A few looks. A couple of hints. They'll soon get the message.' He wrapped up the deal by giving Bonehead's ego a couple of strokes. 'If anybody can do it, you can.'

Bonehead's chest swelled with pride.

'No problem. I'm up for it.'

Jack took in a deep, satisfied breath, and let it out again. Mission accomplished.

'How much?' Bonehead asked, looking businesslike.

'One pound per day,' Jack said, equally businesslike. Bonehead started shaking his head before the words were out of his mouth.

'No way, man. I've got to pay my mates too, haven't I? Two quid.'

'Sorry. Can't afford it.' Jack turned on his heel.

'All right.' Bonehead rushed to stop him. 'One pound eighty.'

'Twenty.'

'Seventy-five.'

'Thirty-five.'

'Sixty.'

'One pound fifty pence, and that's my final offer.' It was what Jack had intended to pay him all along.

'Done,' Bonehead said quickly, and held out his hand. Jack took it gingerly, and they shook.

'Do you want me to start today?' Bonehead asked eagerly. Jack nodded, and took a pound coin and five ten-pence pieces from his pocket. He'd raided his money box before he left that morning.

'There are a couple more things.' Jack handed the money over to Bonehead, who stared at it avidly, as if he'd never seen the coins of the realm in his life until now. 'Don't talk to me in class, or anywhere else about – what we've agreed on just now. Meet me round here by the bins every morning before the bell, and I'll pay you then. Can I trust your mates?'

Bonehead nodded virtuously, his fingers closing over the money like a greedy starfish.

'You can trust them.'

'I hope so. And one more thing . . .' Jack thought hard, and hoped he'd covered all eventualities. 'If any of the teachers find out what's going on, you don't say anything about my sister, understand? You can blame me for putting you up to it, but let me sort it out from there.'

'All right.' Bonehead hesitated, and for a second Jack thought wildly that he was going to add 'Boss'. 'I'd better go and tell my mates.'

'Good.' Jack felt a burst of laughter tickling at his throat, and hastily tried to smother it down. It was probably hysteria anyway. 'My sister will be getting here soon with Nicko. And I'll be watching to make sure everything goes according to plan.'

'It will.' Bonehead turned smartly on his heel, then turned back to attempt what was, for him, a giant leap of the imagination, empathy not being one of his strong points.

'Must be difficult for you. Having a sister who's a nutter, I mean.'

'Yes,' Jack said, fighting down another bout of hysterical giggling. 'It is.'

Bonehead nodded, as if unsure whether or not to say something else. In the end, he simply

141

marched off, looking as if his life now held some purpose. Leaning against the canteen wall, Jack watched him go. Suddenly he didn't feel like laughing any more. Bile rose up in his throat, and for a moment he thought he was going to faint. He slid down the wall into a squatting position, stuck his head between his knees and breathed deeply. Then he waited.

Nicko and Annie came into the playground about half an hour later. There were already quite a few children around by now, and as Jack watched Nicko and Annie come through the gates, he could see that some of them were making remarks, and laughing. He saw Nicko grab Annie's hand, and hustle her away across the playground towards the canteen, where Jack had told him he would be waiting. Then, still watching, Jack saw Bonehead and two of his friends appear from nowhere, and glide silently and menacingly up to the crowd of kids hanging around the gate. Satisfied, Jack turned away.

'Here we are.' Looking pale and harassed, Nicko appeared behind him, clinging on to Annie who was dragging her heels and looking cross.

'I want to go and play with Sarah,' she whined.

'All right.' Jack nodded at her. 'Go and play.'

Nicko stared at him in surprise.

142

'Come on, Sarah,' Annie said happily, and she ran off.

Jack glanced at Nicko. He wasn't looking forward to this. Telling Nicko was almost going to be worse than doing business with Bonehead.

'I don't get it.' Nicko looked bewildered. 'What's going on? Why did you let Annie go off like that? And why were you here so early today anyway? I thought we were supposed to be keeping her away from school as much as possible, so the teachers don't catch on.'

'Look.' Jack pointed out into the playground. Annie had produced a skipping-rope from her pocket, and was chatting animatedly to Sarah as she skipped. There was a large empty space all around her. The closest people to her were Bonehead and one of his mates, who were policing the space at a respectful distance. Another of Bonehead's gang was standing guard at the gate, having a quiet word with the other children as they arrived. None of the children in the playground were now even staring at Annie. They were all studiously looking elsewhere.

Nicko looked even more bewildered.

'They're leaving her alone. Why?'

Jack looked down at his feet.

'I asked Bonehead to sort them out.'

There was silence for a second or two.

'You asked *Bonehead*?' Nicko stuttered.

Jack nodded.

'You asked Bonehead to do WHAT?' Nicko's voice rose several decibels.

'Sssh.' Jack looked round nervously. 'I just asked him to have a quiet word with the kids who are teasing her. No violence,' he added hastily. 'Nothing like that.'

'So what's in it for Bonehead?'

Jack cleared his throat.

'I'm paying him.'

'You're PAYING him?' Nicko could hardly get the words out, his eyes huge dark pools of anger in his white face. 'You're PAYING him?'

'Will you stop repeating everything I say?' Jack snapped. 'What else could I do? I had to stop the teasing somehow.'

'You're running a protection racket. Who do you think you are, Al Capone?' Nicko yelled. 'You can't do this, Jack.'

'I already have,' Jack said miserably. 'I've got to stop Annie from stealing anything else. If she gets caught—'

'I know, I know.' Nicko lifted his shoulders, then let them fall. 'But there's got to be another way. What if *you* get caught? Daniels will rip you to pieces.'

'I've got to take the chance. If I can stop the teasing, Annie will stop stealing.'

144

'Not necessarily. She could carry on doing it anyway.'

'No, she won't. That's not part of the game.'

'What do you mean?'

'It's not part of the game. She's pretending Sarah's the thief. If we stop the other kids teasing her, there's no reason for "Sarah" to nick things off them.'

'But then that means that Annie really believes that it's Sarah, not her, who steals the things.'

'I think she does.' Too late, Jack saw the trap he'd walked into.

'But then . . .' Nicko's brow furrowed. 'That means that Annie really believes in Sarah. She isn't just doing it to wind everybody up, like you said.'

The bell for morning school rang out at that moment. Jack turned away, relieved.

'Come on, let's go in.'

'But, Jack—'

'I don't want to talk about it, all right?' Jack said in a strained voice. 'It's only for the next two weeks, and then we'll be gone.'

Nicko didn't say anything. They both looked across the playground at Annie. She was walking down to the infants' end of the school, hand in hand with Sarah. No-one was near her. The other infants were scuttling along in a huddle, well away from her, with Bonehead and his mates casually bringing up the rear, their eyes darting from side to side.

'It'll be all right,' Jack said quietly. 'You'll see.'

Nicko did not answer. He had a terrible, sick feeling in the very bottom of his stomach.

CHAPTER EIGHT

Jack crossed off the number '3' on his chart. Then he rolled over, and propped the piece of card up against his bedside lamp. There were only two days to go now before they left for America. Only two more days left on his home-made calendar to cross out. Then he would be jetting away from all his problems, leaving all his worries behind. He glanced at his suitcase, standing in the corner. He was packed and ready to go. Nothing could stop him now.

Operation Bonehead had worked beautifully for the last week and a bit, and it was still working. No-one was teasing Annie now; nor had there been any more announcements in

Assembly about the thief. To Jack's intense relief, Annie, and 'Sarah', had been stopped, and the teachers weren't even aware of what was going on. Even Nicko had reluctantly admitted that Jack's bizarre plan had worked. Now it only had to work for two more days, and then they'd be gone.

'Jack?' That was his mum calling from downstairs. 'Time for school. Nicko's here.'

'Coming.' Jack climbed off his bed, giving the chart one last look. Two days. He didn't know what was going to happen when they got back. He'd worry about that when the time came. Somehow he knew, though, that seeing his dad again would help him enormously. It would help him to sort everything out. Help him to get everything straight in his mind. He couldn't wait.

'Jack!' His mother was now sounding distinctly irritated. She hadn't been easy to live with for the last week or so.

Jack went outside to find Nicko and Annie waiting for him in the front garden.

'Not long to go now,' Nicko said as they walked to school. 'You must be getting excited.'

'I am.' Jack felt a band of enormous happiness tighten round his chest. Annie, who was walking along beside him, didn't say anything. Her face looked pale and pinched. Jack glanced at her, and wondered briefly how she was feeling about

148

meeting her father for what was effectively the first time. Perhaps she was nervous. But he pushed the thought away easily. Annie was as tough as old boots. She could cope with anything.

When they arrived at school, Annie skipped off with Sarah, as she did every morning, to play in solitary splendour in one corner of the playground. It was a corner which was now religiously avoided by every other child in the school. Meanwhile, Jack and Nicko slipped away behind the canteen, and waited. A couple of minutes later, Bonehead appeared round the corner, and the daily transaction was completed in silence.

'What're you going to do about Bonehead when you get back from the States?' Nicko asked Jack when Bonehead had gone.

'What do you mean?'

'Well, d'you reckon he's just going to let you stop paying him? He thinks he's got a job for life now.'

'I'll sort it out when I get back,' Jack said, unconcerned. Everything would be all right once he'd seen his father. He just knew it. He hadn't said anything to Nicko, but maybe he wouldn't even come back at all. Maybe his dad would want him to stay there in America with him. It wasn't likely, and Jack wasn't sure how he'd feel about it if his father made the offer, but it was a possibility. There were so many more possibilities, now that his father was back in his life. And he knew one thing for sure. His father was guaranteed to be on his side against Annie.

The morning was an ordinary one, right up until Assembly. As usual, the whole school filed into the hall, and sat there in silence, waiting for the head teacher to appear. As usual, Jack could see Annie sitting at the end of the front row near the doors in the same place she always sat, her legs crossed neatly. He reckoned that she had worked out precisely where to stand when her class queued up to go into Assembly, so that she could make sure there was space for Sarah to sit down next to her. Maybe that should have given him some sort of clue as to what was going to happen. But it didn't.

Mr Daniels came in, and Assembly began as normal. Just as Mr Daniels finished reading a poem about autumn leaves, one of the swing doors was pushed open timidly. A Year One boy put a terrified face round it.

'Come in, Jared,' said Mr Daniels mildly. 'You're a little late today.'

'My mum's alarm clock didn't go off, sir,' Jared squeaked miserably.

'Never mind. Come and sit down.' Mr Daniels' gaze swept up the side of the hall. 'There's a space there, next to Annabel Robinson.'

There was only time for one quick, intense thrill of horror to shudder down Jack's spine, before Jared, dying to curl himself up into the tightest, most insignificant ball he possibly could, rushed over to sit down next to Annie.

'No!' As Jared's bottom was hovering over the empty space next to her, Annie reached out and gave him a violent push. 'You can't sit there!'

Jared staggered. No-one spoke. No-one even gasped. There was a complete and chilling silence in the hall that was the silence of sheer amazement. Jack began to shake all over with fear. Then he felt Nicko's fingers gripping his arm so tightly, he knew that there would be marks there later.

'Don't be silly, Annie,' Mr Daniels said equably. 'Sit down please, Jared.'

Jared looked uncertainly at Annie, his bottom lip starting to tremble.

'He can't sit next to me.' Annie put her arm protectively around the space next to her. 'Sarah's sitting here.'

Jack realized that he was holding his breath, and that if he didn't let it out quite soon, he would suffocate. He breathed out painfully. Then he dared to look across the hall at Mr Daniels, standing quite still in front of them.

He didn't look particularly angry, just rather bewildered.

'Go and sit down next to John Cooper, Jared,' Mr Daniels said quietly. John Cooper was sitting in the next row back, directly behind Annie. Thankfully Jared scuttled to sit down next to him, pulling his knees in tightly to his chest so that they didn't touch the invisible person in front of him.

'Annabel Robinson.' Mr Daniels stared hard at Annie. 'You will stay behind after Assembly.'

Jack wasn't quite sure how he got through the rest of Assembly. He sat there in dumb misery through the songs, and through the notices. When it was time for the children to leave, he sat and watched Miss Turner's class go out first, skirting carefully round Annie, who stayed where she was. One by one the classes filed out. Mrs Reeves' class was last. Jack took one look over his shoulder at his sister's tiny figure, left all alone on the floor in front of Mr Daniels, and groped his way blindly out of the hall.

Nicko too seemed incapable of speech. But all around them the rest of their class was whispering nervously. Not even the threat of Bonehead's intervention could prevent them from discussing the sensational event they had just witnessed. Jack glanced up, and at that moment he caught Bonehead's eye. He could see, too, from the look on the other boy's face that not even the prospect of losing his bodyguard job was going to stop Bonehead himself from making some loud and insulting remark. Jack jumped in first.

'I'll give you an extra quid today if you can stop people going on about you-know-what.'

Bonehead hesitated. 'All right.' Although maybe it wasn't so much the thought of the money that had stopped him from hurling the insult. It was possibly more the rage and misery that was burning in Jack's eyes.

'What happens now?' Nicko didn't find his tongue until they were almost at the classroom door. By mutual, unspoken consent, he and Jack had dropped back in the line to put a distance between themselves and the rest of the class, amongst whom was Bonehead, busily doing his stuff.

'I don't know.' The worst of it was, there was still time for his mother to call the trip off. 'It's up to Daniels. He's going to phone my mum. Or something.'

'Maybe he'll let it go,' Nicko suggested. But he didn't sound too hopeful.

The summons from Mr Daniels came through at ten past three that afternoon, five minutes before the home bell. A Year Three boy, looking supremely inflated with his own importance, bustled into Mrs Reeves' classroom during story time, and handed her a note. Mrs Reeves read it, and her gaze focused on Jack. Before she even read it out, he knew.

'Jack, Mr Daniels would like to see you in his office.'

A subdued murmuring immediately broke out. Jack exchanged one look with Nicko, and went. Mr Daniels was sitting at his desk, his black leather briefcase lying on the table-top. On the briefcase was a long, white envelope.

'I'd like you to give this to your mother, please, Jack.'

Jack reached out and took the envelope. His first feeling was one of overwhelming relief that Daniels hadn't phoned his mum instead. But, before he decided what to do, he had to make sure.

'You could phone her instead, sir,' he said cautiously. 'If you like.'

Mr Daniels shook his head. 'Just give her the letter, please, Jack.'

'Is it about my sister, sir?' Jack couldn't help asking.

'With respect, Jack, I really don't want to discuss this with you.' Mr Daniels stared at him unsmilingly. ' You can go now.'

The envelope burned in Jack's palm as he went back to class. The home bell rang out before he got there, and instead he veered off into the cloakroom, collected his coat and went outside to wait for Nicko. As children streamed out of the building from various exits, almost all of them stared at him with avid curiosity, but no-one said anything. Operation Bonehead was still holding its own remarkably well.

'What did Daniels say?' Nicko rushed out of the school with his jacket half on and half off.

'Not much. He gave me this.' Jack held out the envelope.

'A letter for your mum?' Nicko squinted at it. 'What do you think it says?'

'Something about Annie for sure.' Jack looked grim. 'Something that might stop our trip from going ahead.'

'You'll have to chance it.'

'No, I won't.' Jack glanced around to make sure most of the children had already gone. Then he slid the envelope smoothly down the neck of his sweat shirt. 'Because I'm not going to give it to her.'

'*What?*'

'Not yet, anyway. Not until we get back from seeing my dad.'

Nicko was so shocked, he couldn't speak. He opened and closed his mouth a few times, then gave up. Jack could understand why Nicko was shocked. After all, neither of them had ever been in any real trouble at school before. Now here they were running a protection racket, keeping quiet about thieving and hiding letters from the headmaster. Well, he couldn't help it. He was desperate.

Annie had come out of the Reception classroom, and was marching towards them. When she reached them, though, she didn't stop. She walked straight past, heading for the gate. Jack ran after her, and caught her arm.

'What did Daniels say to you after Assembly this morning?'

Annie shook herself free.

'I don't like him,' she said sullenly. 'I told him about Sarah, and he pretended to believe me, but he didn't really. I hate him.'

She walked off. Jack and Nicko looked at each other, their eyes full of dread.

'She wouldn't,' Nicko said at last. 'Not *Daniels*. Not the *head teacher*.'

'No, of course she wouldn't,' Jack agreed quickly. Stealing from kids was one thing. Stealing from the head teacher was another altogether. All the same, he didn't want to take the risk. 'I'm going to ask my mum if we can have the day off school tomorrow.'

He'd asked her once already, and she'd said no, she didn't want them hanging around the house getting in her way while she tried to finish the packing; there was plenty of time for them to come home from school, get changed and finish packing before they had to leave for the airport. But he'd try again, if only to keep Annie out of trouble on their very last day.

'Good luck.' Nicko cleared his throat. 'Well, if I don't see you again then . . . Have a good time.' He slapped Jack awkwardly on the shoulder.

Jack nodded, without speaking. He felt very tired and, all of a sudden, very scared.

'She said no then.' Nicko's heart sank as he watched Jack and Annie trail gloomily out of their house the following morning. It was a toss-up as to which one looked the most miserable. Nicko had hoped and hoped that Jack would be able to persuade his mother to let him and Annie stay at home today. He didn't think he could take much more of this dangerous game that Jack was playing.

'You got it,' Jack said shortly. His mother hadn't just said no. She'd yelled it, several times. She'd repeated what she'd said before about them getting under her feet. Then she'd packed them off out of the house. He knew that she was on edge because she was getting more and more upset at the prospect of seeing his father again. So much had been going on recently, he had forgotten about his mother's feelings.

'Hello, Annie,' Nicko said nervously.

Annie gave him a look so full of misery that Nicko recoiled. She brushed past him, and went off down the path on her own.

'One more day.' Jack's eyes met Nicko's, and Nicko's met his, and they both recognized the fear there. Neither of them mentioned it, however.

One more day.

As they waited behind the school canteen for Bonehead to appear, Jack kept repeating the comforting phrase to himself. One more day. There wasn't much that could go wrong in one day.

'Where's Bonehead?' he asked suddenly, glancing at his watch. 'He's late.' He'd wondered if it was worth paying Bonehead at all, now that Daniels and the other teachers were fully aware of what was going on, but it was only for one more day, and it wasn't worth the grief that stopping the payments would undoubtedly cause.

As if on cue, Bonehead appeared just then around the dustbins.

'Everything all right?' Jack asked quietly, sliding the money into Bonehead's clammy palm.

Bonehead hesitated. 'Yeah, everything's fine.'

Jack frowned. He'd noticed Bonehead's slight uneasy tone.

'Are you sure?'

'Course I am.' Bonehead shrugged his meaty shoulders. 'It's just that—'

'Just what?' Jack asked, his heart hammering wildly.

'Well, I heard your sister talking to that invisible mate of hers about old Daniels' briefcase a few minutes ago.' Bonehead shook his head in disbelief. 'A bit weird or what?'

Jack lunged forward, and Bonehead stepped back, alarmed.

'What did Annie say about Daniels' briefcase?' Jack demanded, his throat closing up with fear.

'Nothing. She was just talking about it.' Bonehead started edging away. He wasn't frightened of anybody, but when Robinson got that particularly angry gleam in his eyes, it was definitely time to leave.

When Bonehead had gone, Jack and Nicko stared hopelessly at each other without speaking. Annie's conversation with Sarah about the head teacher's briefcase could mean only one thing.

Disaster.

CHAPTER NINE

Jack stood up, and pushed his chair back with a scrape. Around him the rest of the class had their heads bent over their books, reading in silence. Only Nicko was looking up at him, fear and alarm in his eyes. Although he'd never claimed to be telepathic, Jack would have put money on the words running through Nicko's mind right at this moment. 'Don't do it. It's a stupid idea. And it's dangerous.'

'Don't be long, Jack,' said Mrs Reeves as he went over to the door.

'No, miss,' he said dutifully. He went out, closing the classroom door quietly behind him. Then he stopped, and looked casually up and down the corridor. There was no-one around. Jack broke into a run. Keeping his head low, so that the teachers in the adjoining classrooms didn't spot him, he raced for the stairs. He'd asked Mrs Reeves for permission to go to the toilet, which meant he only had about five minutes to make it to Daniels' office and back, before she started becoming suspicious.

Mrs Reeves' classroom was on the ground floor of the school, while Mr Daniels' office was on the second floor. There were two sets of stairs at opposite ends of the school, but one of the staircases, the one that went right up to Mr Daniels' office, was out of bounds for pupils. It was this staircase that Jack was heading for. He'd never broken this particular rule before, but as he was planning to borrow the head teacher's briefcase and hide it somewhere safe before Annie and Sarah Slade got their hands on it, one more lapse of conduct didn't seem to matter much any more.

No-one was around. When Jack, his heart thundering in his ears, was almost at the top of the stairs, he stopped before turning the final corner. The next obstacle he had to negotiate was Mrs Palmer, the school secretary, whose office was next to Mr Daniels'. He could hear her talking on the phone, which probably meant the office door was wide open. Jack risked a quick look round the corner. He could see Mrs Palmer, but she had her back to him. The door to Mr Daniels' office was open too, and that was empty. Jack knew that every Thursday straight after lunch, Mr Daniels took the top two infant classes to read them a story. Hardly stopping to take a breath, he tiptoed up the stairs in a rush, and into Mr Daniels' office.

Relief swept over him as he saw the black leather briefcase open on the desk. So he was in time after all. He hadn't been able to risk coming up here before, knowing that Daniels was likely to be around, but he'd reasoned that Annie would have the same problem. It would be a lot easier for Annie to get out of class though. Everyone knew that infants had to go to the loo every five minutes, whereas it was much harder for the juniors to get away with that excuse.

Jack hurried round the desk, and pushed the lid of the briefcase down. He didn't dare lock it, in case Mrs Palmer next door heard the clicks. Then he picked it up, and slid it under his arm. It was full of papers and folders, and it weighed a ton. He doubted if Annie would be able to pick it up even if she wanted to, but he couldn't take the risk. The briefcase was awkward to hold too, because it wasn't shut properly, so he had to grasp it with both hands. Then he went back over to the door, and peered out cautiously. The secretary was still talking on the phone. Jack eased himself out of the head teacher's office, and ran silently back towards the stairs. A few steps and he'd be round the corner, and halfway down the next bit of the stairs, there was the drama cupboard, which was full of old costumes from school plays. He could hide the briefcase there . . .

'What are you doing, Jack?'

Shocked, Jack stumbled on the last step before the corner. The briefcase slid from under his arm, hit the top of the stairs and bounced back down, showering papers, folders, a mobile phone and a paper bag of jelly babies everywhere. The briefcase itself came to a halt at the bottom of the stairs, right at the feet of the head teacher. Mr Daniels did not look amused.

'Just the boy I wanted to see,' he said thoughtfully. 'I've been overhearing some very interesting gossip about you and Basil Griffiths, and now—' Mr Daniels looked round at the contents of his briefcase, which were littering the staircase like confetti. 'We can also discuss the identity of the school thief.'

Jack walked along beside his mother in silence. Annie was walking along on the other side of her, and she wasn't saying anything either. As they left the playground, Jack glanced back over his shoulder at the school. He knew, with a sinking, certain heart, that tomorrow he would be walking back through those gates, instead of through New York customs to meet his father.

The scene with Mr Daniels in his office was not one that Jack wanted to remember, but he knew that he would, as long as he lived. Mr Daniels had been stern, pleading, threatening and gentle by turn, but Jack had remained dumb. He hadn't known what to say. He hadn't even known where to start. In the end, Mr Daniels had phoned Jack's mother. Jack also wanted to erase from his mind the expression on his mother's face when she'd walked into the head teacher's office, but he knew he wouldn't forget that in a long time either.

He'd been sent outside, while Mr Daniels and his mother had a long chat. Then his mum had come out, looking pale and strained, and said that she was going to take Jack and Annie home right away, even though it was only halfway through the afternoon. No mention was made of the flight they were supposed to be catching later that day. A passing child was ordered to collect Annie from Miss Turner and bring her to Mr Daniels, and when she arrived, they left. A message was also sent to Mrs Reeves to explain Jack's absence. Jack hadn't even had time to say anything to Nicko, who'd probably chewed his book to pieces with worry by now.

The journey home was made in a terrible, sustained silence. By the time they got to the house, Jack's nerves were stretched to their limits.

'Annie, will you go and play upstairs please?' their mother said as soon as they were inside. 'I want to talk to Jack.'

Annie went obediently, without a word. Jack's mother reached over and pushed open the living-room door. She motioned Jack in with a curt nod. His face pale with misery, Jack stumbled past her and into the room. He'd blown everything, big-time, and he knew it.

'I don't know where to start.' His mother shut the door behind her, and turned to face him. 'Where shall I start, Jack?'

'I don't know,' he muttered.

'Well, shall I start with you stealing Mr Daniels' briefcase? Or with you being the school thief? Or with the letter you didn't give me? Or shall I start with the protection racket you and this boy Brickhead have been running?'

'Bonehead.'

'Whatever.' His mother didn't take her eyes from his face. Jack stood in the middle of the room, feeling her anger eddying around him like a whirlpool. 'Jack, what's going on?' She shouted the words at him at first, then she repeated them in a voice that was more dazed than angry. 'What's going on?'

'It's not my fault,' he said in a low voice.

His mother raised her eyebrows.

'Whose fault is it then?'

Jack hesitated. If he took this route, there would be no going back. But what did it matter now? What did anything matter?

'Annie's.'

'Annie's? How can it be *Annie's* fault?'

'It *is* her fault!' Jack yelled, goaded past endurance by the scepticism in his mother's voice. 'It always is!'

'Jack . . . ?'

'It's because of Annie and Sarah Slade that I got myself into this! Don't you understand?'

His mother looked at him. 'I can't understand if you don't tell me.'

There were a few seconds of electrified silence. Then it all came out, in a huge stream that could no longer be dammed. How Annie's game with Sarah Slade had got out of hand. How Annie had been stealing things from the children at school, who were teasing her. The protection racket with Bonehead. Why Daniels' briefcase had become involved. Why he wanted to see his dad so much. How much he blamed Annie for his dad leaving. And how truly terrible it was to have a baby sister who was so much cleverer than he was.

When he finally stopped, there were two different feelings fighting for supremacy inside him. One was a mixture of guilt and fear that he'd finally let all his feelings about Annie to the surface. The other was a giddy sense of relief that everything was now out in the open. As he waited, watching his mother, the feeling of relief grew and grew, smothering the guilt and fear.

'Jack . . .' His mother tried to say something, then stopped, as if she was re-thinking the sentence. Jack wondered, out of everything he'd told her, what she would focus on.

'Jack, what you said about your father leaving because of Annie . . . That's not true.'

Jack looked at her warily.

'It is. I remember what it was like. She was a complete pain.'

'No.' His mother shook her head. 'It had nothing to do with Annie. Your father was going to leave anyway a few years before. Then . . . Then we found out I was expecting Annie, and we decided to give things another go.'

Jack stared at her. No. That wasn't right.

'Things were rocky before Annie came along. Don't you remember?'

He shook his head dumbly, fast-forwarding

through his memories. They were good before Annie was born, bad afterwards. Or had he just been selective?

'I don't believe you,' he said automatically, then was appalled that he'd let the words out of his mouth. His mother wasn't a liar.

'I thought you knew.' His mum put her arm round him, and drew him over to the sofa. Jack sat down automatically. A savage, ruthless pain was searing through him. He'd never have believed that his dad would have left him, unless Annie had driven him away. The shocking realization that his father had been prepared to go anyway numbed him to the core.

'You must remember the rows we had,' his mother went on. 'About money, mostly. That was long before Annie was born.'

Jack thought back. Yes, he remembered the rows. But he hadn't realized how far they'd gone. All this time he'd thought something different, deceived himself . . . He should have been told the truth. Fury and misery struck him dumb, and he pulled away from his mother.

'We should have talked about it.' She reached out tentatively to him, then stopped herself. 'But you seemed to be coping so well with your father going away and not keeping in touch, that I didn't want to rock the boat.' She gave a wry laugh. 'I took the easy way out, I suppose. And it never struck me that you blamed Annie for your father leaving. I thought it was just that you were jealous—' She stopped.

'I was,' Jack said slowly. 'I am.' To be fair to his mother, that had always been part of the problem too. He *was* jealous of Annie. It didn't seem right or natural to him that she was so much younger, and yet so much brighter than he was. The two things – his father leaving and Annie's IQ – had been inextricably linked in his mind. Now he was slowly and painfully beginning to separate the two strands of emotion out, like tangled skeins of wool.

His mother sighed.

'Your dad's a nice man, Jack, but he's got his faults. He's not a hero. And Annie's not the villain of the piece.' Her smile was shaky. 'She's got her faults too, but she's just a little girl.'

Jack stared down at his feet. He was realizing, with a painful pang, that he was now faced with the task of renegotiating two of the most important relationships in his life, one with his father and one with his sister. The first had become more complex, the latter more simple, but they would both need a delicate touch. Neither did he underestimate just how difficult it was going to be to change the pattern of his relationship with Annie, in particular. He hoped it wasn't too late.

'Jack, about Annie.' His mother reached out and took his hand. This time he did not pull away. 'I just want you to know that I've decided to get some help for her. Some real help. The school is doing its best, but it's obviously not enough. All this business with Sarah has shown me that.'

'I'm glad,' Jack said simply.

'Things are going to be different from now on.' His mother smiled. 'Well, let's be honest. I *hope* they're going to be different. I just wish you'd told me what was going on. Then you'd never have got yourself into this mess.'

'What do you think Mr Daniels is going to do to me?' Jack asked nervously.

'Nothing, I hope. I'll have a long chat with him when we get back from seeing your dad.'

'When we get back . . .' Jack's face lit up. 'You mean we're still going?'

'Of course.' His mother gave him a teasing smile. 'I couldn't afford to lose all that money I paid out for the tickets—' she stopped, guilt written all over her face.

'You bought the tickets. Not Dad.' Somewhere at the back of his mind, Jack had always suspected that.

His mother sighed.

'When I phoned your dad back to discuss the visit, he said he'd love to see you but he just didn't have the cash after all. I didn't want you to be disappointed, so . . .'

Jack put his arms round her, and the last bit of anger remaining inside him vanished.

'Well, you'd better go up and finish your packing.' His mother returned the hug, then stood up. 'We've got to leave in a couple of hours. Will you check that Annie's finished hers?'

'All right.' Jack went over to the door. Strangely he felt lighter and even younger, as if a mountain of worry he'd been carrying around on his shoulders had suddenly melted away.

'Annie?' As he went towards his sister's bedroom, Jack felt strangely shy. It was almost as if all the problems of the last four years had suddenly been washed away, and they were ready to make a new start. But he had to be careful. Just because he felt that way, there was no reason why Annie should. To her, Jack was still the grumpy big brother who was carefully uninterested in anything she said or did. It would be up to Jack to change that . . . If he could. Like his mother had said, it wouldn't be easy.

Annie wasn't in her room. That was the first thing Jack noticed. The second thing he noticed was the pile of objects piled neatly on the bed. He could see a baseball cap, a doll, a recorder, and several other children's things. There was also a black diary, with a pair of gold-framed glasses balanced on top. A little to one side, away from the rest of the pile, was a blue instrument case.

Jack ran across the room, and grabbed it. Trembling all over, he flicked back the locks and opened the case. His saxophone gleamed back at him.

Everything that Annie had taken was back. But where was Annie herself? Jack frowned. He hadn't heard her come downstairs while he and his mother were talking.

'Mum!' he shouted. 'Annie's not here.'

'What?' His mother came to the bottom of the stairs, holding a mug of tea. 'She must be. She isn't down here.'

'She isn't.' Pushing a few of the silver buildings aside, Jack knelt down and looked under the bed. Annie wasn't there, and there were no other hiding-places. As he was climbing to his feet, he saw the Sarah Slade plasticine doll, lying on the desk. He went over and picked it up. A sharp fear he could almost taste stabbed him in the heart. There was a second plasticine model too, a girl holding hands with Sarah. The girl had brown curls and big brown eyes, and she was wearing a green dress. It was Annie herself.

CHAPTER TEN

Jack prowled restlessly around the living-room. Every few seconds he lifted up the net curtain, and looked out into the street, to see if his mother was on her way back. She'd gone out in the car to tour the roads round their house to look for Annie. Jack had wanted to go with her, but his mother had told him to wait in the house, in case Annie suddenly turned up. His mother had also said, as she ran out of the house white-faced and wild-eyed, that if she hadn't found Annie within half an hour, she was going to come straight back and call the police.

There was no sound in the house, except the insistent ticking of the clock over the fireplace.

Visions of his sister abducted, hurt, maybe even killed, churned relentlessly through Jack's mind, and he had to rationalize them away. Annie had only been gone for forty minutes, at the most. And she was smart. Much too smart to fall into anyone's trap. Thoughts like these made him feel better for a minute or two. But then all the fears came rushing back, and he had to go through the whole rationalization process again.

Annie had gone – why? That was the question Jack kept on asking himself. Answer – she was unhappy, obviously. Jack felt his insides curl with self-hatred as he realized that he'd probably contributed to that. All he wanted to do now was to try and put things right. But he couldn't do that until Annie came home. If she came home.

To make himself feel that he was doing something useful, Jack searched the whole house again, as thoroughly as possible. When he found himself looking in places like behind the TV set and in the bath, he realized that he'd exhausted every sensible possibility, and went into the kitchen to get himself a drink, just for something to do. The kitchen clock read three fifteen. They were supposed to be leaving for the airport in just over an hour, but Jack was not surprised to find that he didn't care if they missed their plane.

He just wanted Annie to come home. If she didn't, they'd never get the chance to start their relationship all over again. Not only that, he'd feel guilty for ever.

He stood at the window, drinking the glass of Coca Cola he'd poured, although he didn't taste a drop. Their back garden stretched away in front of him. It was long, but there were no hidden places there where Annie might be.

A movement in the garden next door caught the edge of Jack's vision. He slammed his glass down onto the work surface, and leaned over the sink to fling the window open. Then his heart sank. It was only Jeffrey, their next-door neigh- bour's black-and-white cat, strolling down the gravel path, waving his tail from side to side like a pennant. Jack watched him walk the length of the path, and draw sinuously to a halt outside the neighbour's shed. His sister loved that cat. She wanted one herself, but their mother was allergic to the fur—

Jack's whole body stiffened. He was still watching Jeffrey, who was sniffing round the shed, and miaowing. Then he saw the cat start scrabbling frantically at the bottom of the shed door.

Jack was out of the kitchen in a second. He grabbed the key to the back door, dropping it twice as he tried to get it into the lock, and fumbling with the stiff bolts. Then he was out in the back garden. He gave the house next-door only the briefest glance before climbing over the low fence between the two gardens. He didn't think there was anyone home, but anyway, Lucy, their neighbour, was a good friend of his mother's, and he knew she wouldn't mind. Not in the circumstances.

Jeffrey gave a small squeak of recognition as Jack ran down the path towards him. This turned into a squeal of protest, as Jack picked him up and moved him unceremoniously away from the shed door. Deeply offended, Jeffrey stalked away with his nose in the air, and sat down vindictively in the middle of Lucy's vegetable patch. Jack didn't take any notice. He pulled the shed door open.

Annie was curled up on an old sack in the corner. She looked up, startled, as Jack burst in, knocking over a garden rake and a pile of plant pots.

'Annie!' Overjoyed at finding her, Jack ran forward. He had some confused idea of throwing his arms around her, but the mutinous look on Annie's face, and the way she shrank back against the wall of the shed, stopped him cold. 'Annie, what are you doing here?'

'Thinking.' Annie stared up at him defiantly. 'I needed somewhere to think.'

'You shouldn't have gone out like that.' Jack squatted down beside her. He felt utterly light-headed with relief. 'Mum's driving round like a madwoman looking for you.'

Annie didn't say anything. She just continued to stare at her brother with wide, grave eyes. Jack began to feel slightly uncomfortable, and all the old, familiar feelings of annoyance surged up inside him. But he'd warned himself already that things weren't going to be easy, hadn't he? He had to make an effort.

'Come on.' He held out his hand. 'We'd better get back before Mum calls the police.'

'No.' Annie shook her head.

Jack looked at her blankly.

'Don't be daft.'

'I'm not. I don't know yet if I'm coming back or not.'

Jack bit back the angry words that sprang to his lips. 'Where do you think you'll go instead?'

Annie looked at the empty space next to her.

'Sarah wants me to go with her.'

'Back to the twenty-fifth century?' Jack knew now that his sister really believed in Sarah. She'd conjured her up in a desperate bid for a friend, and now Sarah was as real to Annie as he was. Maybe even more so.

Annie nodded. 'Sarah's going home today, and

she's asked me to go with her. Not for a visit. For ever.'

Jack stared at her. Some instinct inside his head was telling him, in an authoritative voice that could not be ignored, that whatever he said now would determine the pattern of their relationship for the rest of their lives.

'You don't want to go, do you?'

'I don't know. I might.'

'No, you don't,' Jack persisted. 'What about Mum? She loves you. She'd be devastated.'

Annie looked down at the sack she was sitting on. Her fingers pulled insistently at a loose thread.

'I know. But she might be glad, in a way.' She looked solemnly at Jack. 'Then she wouldn't have to worry about me any more.'

'Well, what about me?' Jack said stubbornly. 'I don't want you to go either.'

There was a long silence. For once, Annie didn't know what to say. There was a ring of truth in her brother's voice, but after almost five years of division, she couldn't believe that he meant what he said.

'But you don't like me.' It didn't come out as an accusation. Just as a statement of fact. 'You've never liked me.'

'Don't be silly. You're my *sister*.' But Jack could hear the bluster in his own voice.

Annie shrugged, and said nothing.

'All right.' The time for plastering over the cracks in their relationship was now finished. 'I was jealous of you.'

Annie looked genuinely puzzled.

'Jealous of me? Why?'

'Because . . .' Jack had to struggle to force the confession out. 'Because you're cleverer than I am. Much cleverer. And you're only a kid.'

'Oh, that.' Annie shrugged again. 'It's not much to be jealous of really.' She looked down at the loose thread, and pulled it hard. 'Why do you want to be as clever as me anyway? Nobody likes me.'

'Don't be silly.'

'They don't.' Annie focused her clear, candid gaze on her brother. 'Nobody likes you if you're different. It's easier if everyone's the same.'

Jack couldn't think of anything to say.

'I'm jealous of *you*,' Annie said. 'You've got loads of friends, and I haven't. Well, except for Sarah.'

'I didn't think you wanted to have loads of friends. You seemed happy on your own.'

'I'm not.' Annie's voice wobbled. 'But I don't know *how* to be friends.'

'What about the kids in your class?'

'Oh, *them*. They all say that I talk about stupid things, and that they don't understand what I'm

179

on about.' Annie looked miserably up at her brother. 'But I don't know how to talk about anything else.'

'Well, you don't have to be friends with them,' Jack said encouragingly. 'There are plenty of other people around.' He was beginning to get an inkling now of how the Sarah Slade game had been born, out of his sister's isolation and vulnerability. 'There are lots of other kids like you. You're not the only one, you know.'

Annie looked at him doubtfully. Then she turned her head as if she was seeking advice from Sarah.

'Mum's going to sort it out,' Jack persisted. 'Come on, Annie, it's worth a try, isn't it?'

Again he held out his hand. Annie hesitated.

'What's the matter?' Jack asked.

'I think . . .' Annie looked away. 'I think I might go with Sarah. She really wants me to, you know.'

'But Mum and I really want you to stay,' Jack said urgently.

'Yes, but if I stay with you and Mum, then . . .' Annie's voice tailed away.

'Then what?'

'If I stay here, then I have to go to America,' Annie muttered, looking down at her feet.

'You mean you don't want to go to America?' Jack stared at her, perplexed. This whole situation had gone deeper than he would ever have thought possible. 'Why not?'

Annie avoided his gaze, still staring at her feet and muttering. Jack just managed to catch the word 'Dad'.

'You're worried about seeing Dad again?' he deduced slowly.

Annie nodded.

'Why?'

'He won't like me.'

'He's your father, of course he'll like you,' Jack said, amazed. 'Why shouldn't he?'

'Why should he? You're my brother, and *you* don't like me.'

That took the breath out of Jack like a punch to the stomach. He squatted down in front of his sister again, searching for words to reassure her.

'Annie, he'll like you. I promise.'

Annie looked unconvinced. With a sudden flash of insight, Jack realized that he was once again making the mistake of treating Annie like an ordinary five-year-old. Reassurance was not enough. She needed an explanation. She needed facts.

'Annie, listen to me. I think Dad's going to love you, but that's not the point. Even if he doesn't, it doesn't matter. Dad isn't really part of our lives any more, and he isn't going to be ever again . . .' Jack realized painfully that he was speaking as much to himself as he was to Annie. 'He walked out on us, and we're the ones who matter now. You, me and Mum. And me and Mum want you to stay . . .'

His voice tailed away. Had he done enough to persuade her?

There was silence for a few moments. Then Annie climbed to her feet. She turned away from Jack, and spoke to the air next to her.

'I can't go with you, Sarah. I'm sorry.'

Jack shook all over with relief. He held out his hand for a third time.

'Come on, Annie. Time to go.'

'Goodbye, Sarah.' Annie stared intently at the empty space in front of her. 'You've been my *best* friend. I'll never forget you.'

She put out her arms as if she was hugging someone, and then stood quite still in the invisible embrace for a long time. Jack felt a lump unexpectedly rise up in his throat.

'I hope you get home safely.' Annie reached out and finally took her brother's hand. 'Bye, Sarah.'

'Let's go,' Jack said gently, and they went out into the garden hand in hand.

CHAPTER ELEVEN

Jack turned round in his very small seat, trying to get comfortable. The steady drone of the aeroplane engines was making him drowsy, but the large American man who was squashed into the seat next to him as tightly as a cork in a bottle meant that Jack couldn't get settled. They had already apologized to each other politely for clashing elbows several times.

Jack glanced to his left. Annie was already fast asleep in the seat across the aisle. She was snuggled under Jack's coat, and just the tip of her head could be seen. Their mother was in a seat a couple of rows in front. Because of the delay caused by searching for Annie, they'd been very late checking in and they hadn't managed to get seats all together. The cabin lights had been dimmed, and almost everyone around him was asleep too.

Jack turned his head to stare out at the blue-black darkness outside. He wished he could have got a window seat, but then again, maybe not. The woman who was asleep there looked even more squashed than he did. She'd started off the journey trying to knit because she said it calmed her nerves, but had to give up when her wool got caught in the American man's watch strap. They'd all got so engrossed in trying to untangle it, that Jack didn't even realize that the plane had taken off.

He closed his eyes. He was almost halfway to his father by now. The thought still sent excitement rushing through him, but it was a different kind of excitement from what he'd been feeling before. Then he'd been desperate for some kind of solution to his problems. Now he had the answers, and he knew, with a sad wisdom, that his father couldn't have given him the solutions he needed, anyway. He was going to enjoy seeing his father again, but then he was going to come home and get on with his real life once more. A real life that included his sister, fabulous IQ, and all. Jack was too intelligent to expect that he and Annie would become best friends overnight. Maybe they'd never become best friends at all. But already he had noticed a lightening of their relationship, a gradual shrugging-off of the roles that they'd accepted for themselves over the last five years.

'Pardon me, son.' Jack yelped, and shot bolt upright as the man next to him stood up, and trod on his toes. 'I wonder if I might just squeeze past you.'

Yawning, Jack squashed himself into as small a ball as he possibly could, drawing up his knees to his chin, so that the man could get past him. He lumbered off down the aisle towards the lavatory, and Jack wondered sleepily if the airline had rules about the maximum weight each passenger could be, and what would happen to the plane if every passenger was the same size as the American man . . . His eyelids drooped again. There wasn't much point in going back to sleep, because the man would be back soon, and they'd have to go through the whole rigmarole all over again. But he was so tired . . .

'Hello, Jack.'

Jack looked up. He thought it was one of the air stewardesses speaking to him, but it wasn't. It was a girl of about his own age with long blond hair. She smiled at him.

'Don't you recognize me, Jack? It's me. Sarah.'

It was then that Jack knew he was asleep. He'd

185

had these kind of dreams before, when he was actually dreaming a vivid dream on one level of his mind, but on another, he knew quite clearly that he was asleep. The choice he had now was whether to wake himself up and let it go, or whether to dream on.

'Hello, Sarah,' he said faintly.

'Can I sit down?' Sarah pushed her way lightly past Jack's knees, and sat down in the empty middle seat.

'Someone's sitting there,' he said.

Sarah shrugged.

'Don't worry. I jammed the lavatory door. He won't be back for a few minutes.'

She smiled at Jack again.

'So, we meet at last,' Sarah said. 'I didn't want to leave without saying goodbye to you. Even though you did ruin all my plans.'

'What plans?'

'To take Annie back home with me.' Sarah smiled ruefully. 'I would have looked after her, you know. She would have been happy.'

'She's happy here with Mum and me,' Jack said.

'Maybe. But we would have respected her intelligence, and used it to its maximum potential. Here, most people treat her as if she's some kind of problem.'

'That's going to change,' Jack said firmly.

Sarah raised her eyebrows.

'Do you really believe that?'

'Yes,' Jack said sharply.

Sarah shrugged. 'Good luck. You're going to need it. I still think you should have let her come with me.'

Jack wasn't going to let her get away with that.

'Did you really come here to do research, or did you just want Annie all the time?'

'That's sharp of you.' Sarah looked at him appreciatively. 'Yes, it was Annie I wanted.'

Jack felt a wave of anger sweep over him.

'So you pretended to be her friend. And all that stuff with the stealing—'

'Divide and conquer.' Sarah nodded. 'I wanted her to trust me, and no-one else.' She sighed. 'She almost did, in the end. But by that time I was fond of her too. She's an amazing person.'

'You nearly got what you wanted though.' Jack's voice shook with anger. 'You nearly took her away.'

'Don't judge me, Jack. You don't know why.'

'I know you nearly kidnapped my sister!'

'It would never have been by force,' Sarah said calmly. 'She would have had to agree whole-heartedly. We're not evil, Jack. Just desperate. You don't know what it's been like since—' she stopped.

'Since what?'

Sarah shook her head.

'I can't tell you the future, Jack. That would be dangerous.'

'Why are you so keen to take people like Annie back to your own time with you, anyway?' Jack persisted. 'What do you want them for?'

Sarah said nothing.

'Does something happen?' Jack asked urgently. 'Some kind of holocaust?'

'Stop it, Jack.' Sarah gave him a warning look. 'I can't tell you that.'

'Well, can you tell me if everything between Annie and me is going to be all right?' he smiled at her. 'You owe me that much.'

'I can't tell you anything.' Sarah smiled back at him. 'But you're doing all right so far, aren't you?' She rose gracefully to her feet. 'Goodbye, Jack. You won't see me again.'

'Wait a minute,' Jack said quickly, but already he could feel the dream fading away. He struggled awake, and opened his eyes.

'Pardon me again, son.' The large American was standing by the row of seats. 'I need to sit down.'

'Sorry,' Jack muttered dazedly. He drew his knees up to his chin again, and let the man pass. The dream had been so vivid, he still felt disorientated.

The woman sitting by the window was also awake now, and the American turned to her.

'I got locked in the john, would you believe,' he said, taking out a handkerchief and wiping his red face. 'Took them five minutes to get me out.'

Jack's heart began to beat thunderously, roaring in his ears like the sea. It was a coincidence, of course.

Across the aisle, Annie stirred. She sat up, pushing the coat off, and looked over at Jack.

'Oh,' she said in a disappointed voice. 'I thought Sarah was here. But I think it was just a dream.'

Jack stared at her. The dream was vivid inside his head, and yet it wasn't a dream. Now he wasn't sure what he believed. He wasn't even sure if it mattered any more. He held his hand out across the aisle, and Annie took it. They held hands there in silence until a stewardess came along with the drinks trolley, and they had to let go.

THE END

HARRIET'S HARE
Dick King-Smith

*All of a sudden, the hare said, loudly
and clearly, 'Good morning.'*

Hares don't talk. Everyone knows that.
But the hare Harriet meets one morning in
a corn circle in her father's wheatfield is a
very unusual hare: a visitor from the far-off
planet Pars, come to spend his holidays on
Earth in the form of a talking hare. Wiz, as
Harriet names her magical new friend, can
speak any language, transform himself into
any shape – and, as the summer draws to
its close, he has one last, lovely surprise
in store for Harriet . . .

WINNER OF
THE 1995 CHILDREN'S BOOK AWARD

**'Weaves fantasy and reality in a
beguiling novel . . . a thoroughly
satisfying read'**
Books for Your Children

ISBN 0440 863406

Now available from all good book stores

CORGI YEARLING BOOKS

BAD GIRLS
Jacqueline Wilson

*Kim's gang had better watch out! Because
Tanya's my friend now, and she'll show them*

Mandy has been picked on at school for as
long as she can remember. That's why she is
delighted when cheeky, daring, full-of-fun
Tanya picks her as a friend. Mum isn't
happy – she thinks Tanya's a BAD GIRL
and a bad influence. Mandy's sure Tanya
can only get her out of trouble, not
into it . . . or could she?

Also available:
THE BED AND BREAKFAST STAR
BURIED ALIVE!
CLIFFHANGER
DOUBLE ACT
GLUBBSLYME
THE LOTTIE PROJECT
THE MUM-MINDER
THE STORY OF TRACEY BEAKER
THE SUITCASE KID

ISBN 0 440 863562

Now available from all good book stores

CORGI YEARLING BOOKS

THE LOTTIE PROJECT
Jacqueline Wilson

I don't want to do a boring old project.
Who wants to be like everyone else?
I'm doing a diary . . .

Hi! I'm Charlie (Don't call me Charlotte –
ever!). History is boring, right? Wrong!
The Victorians weren't all deadly dull and
drippy. Lottie certainly isn't. She's eleven –
like me – but she's left school and has a
job as a nursery maid. Her life is really
hard, just work work work, but I bet she'd
know what to do about my mum's awful
boyfriend and his wimpy little son. I bet she
wouldn't mess it all up like I do . . .

'Vivid, superbly observed story of real life'
THE TIMES

ISBN 0 440 86366X

Now available from all good book stores

CORGI YEARLING BOOKS